STRICTLY PRIVATE
BUSINESS

Strictly Private Business

by

Michael Cronin

Dales Large Print Books
Long Preston, North Yorkshire,
BD23 4ND, England.

British Library Cataloguing in Publication Data.

Cronin, Michael
    Strictly private business.

    A catalogue record of this book is
    available from the British Library

    ISBN   978-1-84262-804-1 pbk

First published in Great Britain in 1975
by Robert Hale & Company

Copyright © Michael Cronin 1975

Cover illustration © Wessel Wessels by arrangement with
Arcangel Images

The moral right of the author has been asserted

Published in Large Print 2011 by arrangement with
Watson, Little Ltd.

Dales Large Print is an imprint of Library Magna Books Ltd.

Printed and bound in Great Britain by
T.J. (International) Ltd., Cornwall, PL28 8RW

ONE

Very seldom in his life had Sam Harris been under the dire necessity of taking a job and working for his bread like any honest citizen. His world was of quite another sort, where you had to sniff around for the right opportunity and grab it smartly, and then move on to the next offering.

He had tried most things and sometimes he had come up lucky; there had also been the sad times when matters had become unglued and the Law had felt his collar and temporarily deprived him of freedom of movement, an occupational hazard that Sam did not dwell on too much since none of his police record was of recent date.

He was a few years over forty, but liked to imagine that he could look no more than thirty-five, or even less on a good day and in the right gear. Dapper, that was the way he thought of himself. Sharp and very quick on the uptake. Nobody's mug.

One of his regrets was that he didn't have much of a physique, but he reckoned he more than made up for it by his fertile brain and his knack at seeing further round a corner than most operators. He almost never took a chance, and if the scene looked like getting rough he would take off at speed with little regard for any unlucky collaborator, which made him a tricky man to have as a partner. You had to watch him all the time, and even then he might diddle you.

He had sandy hair with a natural crinkle. He had tried wearing it at a trendy length, but he looked too much of a Jessie with ginger curls brushing his shoulders, so he had gone back to a normal hair length; his sandy moustache he kept trim and neat.

All in all, and if you didn't know him, he expected to convey the impression of alert prosperity, with just maybe a touch of the gentleman when the object in view was female, as it frequently was.

He had been married once upon a long time ago, but his spouse had given him the elbow pretty sharply when she found that he was perfectly happy to let her support him most of their short period of togetherness. Since then he had been looking for the woman who would be willing and able to support him in the style to which he would like to have been accustomed, and in spite of a number of personal disasters he remained incurably optimistic. A widow with capital, for instance, would suit him fine, if the capital could be got at and the widow wasn't an old bag and past performing.

In the interim, which was now stretching

longer and longer, he took note of whatever talent might come his way, and the sight of a promising pair of legs still had the power to draw him along, occasionally into situations fraught with peril and personal discomfort – some of these younger birds knew they could do better than this ginger-headed git who wasn't all that much of a riot in bed, or a big spender either.

With a few of the older women his average improved if the conditions were right – she had to be soft enough not to see that he was on the make, and in the position to show gratitude for his attentions. Sam was never insulted by the offer of a cash advance to tide him over a sticky patch, nor would he refuse a little present with a marketable value.

As far as possible he lived on credit, and over the years he had developed an extra sense that warned him when his credit was running thin, then he might pay over a token piece of cash as proof of his solvency or move along smartly elsewhere. It was usually the latter since parting with cash grieved him.

Not at all a lovable rogue, an operator with few scruples and little in the way of conventional morals, but with plenty of the old bounce, that was Sam Harris. Scratching for a living of sorts but strictly on his own terms, and forever expecting to run up against the good times which had to be just around the next corner.

He was currently located in a furnished place in Clapham, nothing stupendous, but adequate for his purposes. He had paid a month's rent, and reckoned it was going to be a good investment because he had already begun to sleep with his landlady fairly regularly. Lily was divorced, some ten years his senior and a bit scrawny without her clothes, but after a couple of gins she went like a ball of fire in bed. Every home comfort and maybe there wouldn't be any rent to pay next month.

When Lily told him she had let the small room across the landing to a Mr Cater who had been abroad and had just come back, Sam thought nothing of it because he was the boy in possession and Lily thought he was respectable. Something in the business line, you know, nice and vague to explain his irregular comings and goings.

Then the first time he caught sight of the new lodger walking down the front path he knew it had to be Percy Cater, with those sloping shoulders and sad expression and the way he dragged his left leg – Percy had fallen off a high wall where he had no business to be and the leg had never been right after that. Percy blamed the prison hospital for leaving him so easily identifiable, and for the consequent reduction in his speed.

Sam was also remembering the details that had rendered Percy unavailable in the last couple of years, and they had nothing to do with being abroad, unless the Scrubs counted as foreign territory. There had been the untimely arrival of a security guard and one of those nasty Alsatian dogs when Percy had been once more engaged on his unlawful efforts on a safe – he had actually cracked it and was on the point of helping himself when the job came undone good and proper.

It was widely agreed by all whose opinion mattered that Percy deserved better luck, because he was one of the few old-fashioned craftsmen when it came to coaxing a safe open.

Sam had never reckoned himself in Percy's league; he just didn't have the skill or the finesse, and he knew it. He had done his share of breaking-and-entering, but his technique had been crude compared with Percy's touch. Like himself, Percy worked alone, but in Percy's case it was from choice, while Sam had done his best from time to time to latch on to one of the organised outfits with the big money and the sophisticated gear; but he had never stayed on the payroll long – they always found him too unreliable and temperamental when the going got rough. And he didn't take orders very well. So he had to paddle along by himself.

Now he wondered what Lily would do if he told her about her new lodger, and he wondered still more what she would do if Percy told her about the real Sam Harris and how he got a crust. That would be a pity, it might well ruin a cosy little set-up, and Sam wasn't ready to fold his tent just yet.

A little private conference with Percy was the first priority, to warn him to keep his trap shut for their mutual benefit. Lily steamed out to do her morning's shopping while he was watching from the window. From the back you'd never think she was on the wrong side of fifty. Her legs were all right, she didn't move badly, and she didn't try to dress like a dolly. When the light was out there was still some good mileage to be got out of Lily. All things being equal, Sam seldom refused a free ride.

When Percy came back he had a folded newspaper under his arm, and Sam was remembering that Percy had always been a heavy plunger on the horses – with disastrous luck. In his best days he had pulled off some really lovely jobs, and he should have had plenty stacked away, but the bookies had kept him scratching. So now here he was, in Lily's back room. No wonder he had that sad look.

Sam let him settle in and then went across the landing and rapped smartly on the door.

Percy was in no hurry to open up, and his face did not brighten at the sight of Sam.

'What do you want?' he said in a quite unfriendly fashion.

'That's no way to greet an old mate,' said Sam. He thrust his way into the room and Percy had to back off to avoid being elbowed; he had never been a physical type and Sam and taken him by surprise.

'You're no mate of mine,' said Percy. 'I don't need you, Sam Harris, and that's a fact.'

Sam broke the good news. 'We're neighbours.'

'You mean you live here?' The sadness in Percy's face deepened.

'That's right,' said Sam. He selected a chair. The choice was limited: one armchair and one kitchen chair. He took the armchair.

'Make yourself at home,' said Percy bitterly. 'I do get some lousy luck.'

Sam grinned. 'What's the climate been like abroad, Percy? Our landlady tells me you've been in foreign parts.'

'Get knotted.' Percy sat in the kitchen chair and gazed balefully at Sam.

Sam inspected the room. There was an unmade bed in one corner, a few sticks of old furniture, and a depressing view of Lily's back yard. There were newspapers spread over the table.

'Still picking the losers, I see,' said Sam

conversationally. 'I hope you'll be comfortable here, Percy.'

'I'll manage. You been here long?'

'Nearly long enough,' said Sam. 'She thinks I'm straight and I get home comforts – you might say I've got both feet in the door.'

'You always were a conniving bastard.' Percy sounded more discouraged than ever.

'I'm getting my share,' said Sam, smug and superior. 'You'll keep your trap shut, Percy, or I might tell the old bird your last address, and you'll be out on your ear.'

'I got enough grief without you butting in,' said Percy.

'I heard,' said Sam. 'Your wife did a flit while you were inside, that's rough, Percy.'

'Women!' said Percy. 'I'm well rid of that one, she was a cow. Before she nipped off she sold every scrap we had in the place, right down to the bare bleeding boards, left me strapped, she did.'

Sam shook his head in sympathy. Percy Cater, the walking disaster area. Nothing to show now for all the jobs he had done, jobs which Sam would never have had the nerve or the know-how to tackle.

'If you're all that short, Percy,' he said, 'I can see you right for a bit.'

Percy looked at him with evident suspicion. He knew Sam's reputation.

'You trying to con me, Sam Harris?'

14

'It's a straight offer,' said Sam, not insulted. 'I just don't like to see a bloke with your talent getting a raw deal.'

'You surprise me,' said Percy.

'I surprise myself sometimes. You got any plans, Percy? Anything lined up?'

'Give us a chance,' said Percy. 'I only got out three days back. I don't know what the form is these days. I've had the welfare narks on my back – they offered to see me in a job, living in one of them hostels all nice and tidy.'

'Rehabilitation,' said Sam. 'Make an honest citizen of you, Percy.'

'That's a laugh,' said Percy. 'How are you making out, Sam?' Percy's tone was distinctly more friendly.

'I'm not worrying,' said Sam. 'Nothing too big lately, you know how it goes.'

'Too bloody true I do,' said Percy with feeling.

'Plenty of ideas though,' said Sam. 'You never know what might come along. I like to keep an open mind.'

'It's the only way,' said Percy. 'Opportunity, that's what you look out for all the time.'

'I couldn't have put it better myself,' said Sam.

'That old biddy who runs this place, she's okay?'

Percy was beginning to nibble.

'She knows nothing,' said Sam. 'We'll keep

15

it that way, right?'

'Be a long time before I trust another woman,' said Percy. 'Sam, are you making me a proposition?'

'I never heard that you worked with a partner,' said Sam. 'Would you consider it?'

'Have to think about it,' said Percy.

'I don't have your touch,' said Sam. 'I'll be the first to admit as much, but I don't waste my time when I'm moving around, Percy boy, and I'm not exactly stupid.'

'I never thought you were.' Percy could have made it sound more cordial, but that would have been foreign to his nature, and furthermore he knew what a tricky character Sam was.

In normal circumstances the idea of taking Sam Harris as a partner would have provoked nothing but derision from Percy. Percy had some professional pride; he had a skill that a con-merchant and petty chiseller like Sam Harris could never expect to equal.

But Percy's current situation was perilous, and he had less than fifty quid to call his own and no gear, and even a craftsman as good as Percy needed the right gear to do a proper job.

'Safe information,' said Sam, 'that comes expensive. Everything has jumped sky-high since you were around, Percy.'

'You don't have to tell me,' said Percy. 'Everybody has their hand out, the greedy bastards – nobody trusts anybody.'

From the way he said it Sam guessed that Percy had been looking up his old contacts and that he had been getting a frosty reception: they'd want cash and it seemed Percy was short of cash. So Percy was open to an offer.

Sam decided not to rush things. He stood up. 'I have one or two prospects in mind,' he said. 'We could talk about them sometime or other, Percy – no hurry.'

'We'll do that,' said Percy, not too happily.

'In the meantime I'll put in the good word for you with our landlady, tell her what a nice feller her new lodger is.' Sam grinned expansively and let himself out. Percy was hooked.

Prudently Sam allowed a couple of days to pass before making his next move, just long enough to have Percy feeling that his mode of life needed a lot of improving, since he wasn't being provided with board, just the modest lodging without any frills – not even a telly to pass the lonely evenings, and he had to go out for all his food. Whereas Sam Harris had his feet under Lily's substantial table three times per day and a welcome to her bed whenever he had the inclination.

One evening as Percy was on his way out to buy himself a meager supper in one of the cafés, Sam intercepted him, and Percy needed little persuading when Sam invited him to a meal in a restaurant; Lily was visiting her married sister in Kingston and would stop the night – her absence was important for what Sam had in mind, because he expected to be out late with Percy, and there wouldn't have to be any explanations – Lily had begun to show a possessive interest in Sam's movements, so he knew it was nearly time to be folding his tent.

He bought Percy a steak dinner with all the garnishings and a bottle of plonk, and they didn't talk any business until they had finished.

Then Percy said, 'Okay, Sam, let's have it.'

'I'll show you,' said Sam.

Sam's car was a blue Viva, not yet paid for by any means, but hire purchase was something Sam never lost any sleep over. It was like owing money to a bank and banks, like finance companies, could afford it.

They drove for over an hour and Percy appeared to have gone asleep because he asked no questions, and if he was interested in their destination he kept it to himself. The original sad sack.

Sam took them to one of the new housing developments. There were acres of bungalows and chalets and semis and pricey detached houses with two-car garages.

Percy stirred himself and gazed at their surroundings without favour.

18

'Boy, you must be crazy,' he said. 'You'd need a furniture van to lift enough stuff here to make it worth the journey … not my line at all.'

'We're not after carpets or television sets,' said Sam. 'You wait, Percy, I'll show you something, and I give you my word you won't turn up your nose at it.'

They drove slowly through the shopping area. They came to a building that stood on its own; a flickering neon sign proclaimed that it was *Bernie's Place*; there were cars parked on the tarmac at the sides and in the larger space at the rear, and as they went slowly past they heard the sounds of merriment – the thumping of music and bursts of applause.

Sam stopped some few yards down the road. 'That's it.'

Percy said nothing, just looked back.

'That's no ordinary boozer,' said Sam. 'It's run like one of those clubs up North, and there's nothing else like it around here – drinks and grub and some of the top performers. They pack them in night after night, Percy, and they're all spending money. Strippers, singers, blue comics, the lot. I spent a couple of evenings in there, just watching the business building up, and I tell you it shook me to see all that cash floating about. So I started to nose around a little.'

Percy looked almost interested. 'So?'

'It could be done,' said Sam. 'I can arrange for some inside help. We'd have to give him a small slice of the cake afterwards, but there'll be plenty for you and me.'

'I'll have to hear a lot more,' said Percy. 'I don't fancy bringing in a third party.'

'Stainer's okay,' said Sam. 'He's the senior supervisor, he more or less runs the place and he knows all the angles. He'll give us the inside dope we couldn't get any other way.'

'Maybe,' said Percy with little enthusiasm. 'I still don't like it. I never worked a three-handed job. How far have you taken it with this bloke?'

'Preliminary discussions only,' said Sam. 'I'm no mug. Nothing firm yet, but it looks good to me, and Stainer needs some quick money.'

'Don't we all? What's this job supposed to be worth?'

'According to Stainer,' said Sam, 'there ought to be over four thousand after a good Friday or Saturday night, all used money they could never trace – maybe more if we wait until they have one of the top stars booked. I thought we'd do an even split, you and me.'

'And Stainer? How much does he expect?'

'I sort of promised him five hundred, when we pull it off,' said Sam.

'Sort of,' said Percy heavily.

Sam grinned and shrugged. 'There could be a little slip-up, afterwards. He's an amateur, Percy.'

'That's what scares me,' said Percy. 'You have to trust him and that means we stick our necks out, and that's never a good business.'

'I'll tie the details up nice and tidy,' said Sam. 'There won't be any leak from Stainer. He's got itching fingers, Percy, and he's ready to be bent if he sees the chance.'

'Don't tell him anything he shouldn't know,' said Percy. 'Like where you live, for instance. Has he seen this car?'

'Percy,' said Sam, 'do me a favour—'

—'Okay, okay,' said Percy, 'I just like to make sure we're covered. What else do you know about this feller Stainer?'

'Enough,' said Sam. 'He'd never fool me. He used to work in a joint in Greek Street, that's when I first met him. He didn't amount to anything then, and he doesn't now. Strictly small-time.'

Percy was looking at Sam, and he was thinking that Sam might have been describing himself.

'You're not just giving me a line of talk, are you, Sam?' said Percy. 'I don't have the time to fiddle about with something that isn't going to pay off.'

'I already invested fifty in Stainer as a sweetener,' said Sam. 'Doesn't that prove something? I don't toss half centuries around regardless.'

'Your money,' said Percy.

'A working expense,' said Sam. 'Half of it will come off your share of the split.'

Percy almost smiled. Sam was running true to form.

'You fix up a meeting,' said Percy. 'I'm not saying I'm going to be interested, not until I hear a lot more detail – I never trust an inside job unless I've looked all round it myself. I have to get in there and crack a safe, right?'

Sam nodded, he was about to say something when Percy raised his hand and continued: 'That's a new building, there'll be efficient alarms probably hooked in to the nearest police station, right again? And the safe won't be any old piece of ironmongery waiting to be blown by the first ambitious bloke who stumbles over it – correct me if I'm wrong.'

'Right all through,' said Sam. 'But don't forget we'll have all the information we need from Stainer, that makes the difference, doesn't it? We won't be going in there cold or blind, Percy–'

–'A Soho chiseller,' said Percy, 'we have to rely on trash like that.'

'So you want to forget it?' said Sam. 'Got cold feet already, Percy?'

Percy stared at him and Sam knew he had

made a bad mistake.

'Just a little joke, Percy,' he said. 'No offence.'

'There's never been anything wrong with my nerve,' said Percy. 'Now you listen to me, Sam Harris – if I wasn't in a bit of a jam I wouldn't be sitting here with the likes of you, listening to your smart talk. So let's have no more of the funny jokes. Busting that place isn't like lifting stuff off a Woolworth's counter, which is about your mark from all I ever heard.'

'Simmer down, boy,' said Sam placatingly. 'You're the expert, I know that.'

'You never cracked a safe in your life,' said Percy with open contempt. 'If I decide to do it we'll split sixty-forty and I get the long end.'

Sam smiled, which was not what he felt like doing. 'Like you just said, there's nothing wrong with your nerve, Percy. Okay, we'll do it your way.'

He started the car and they drove for half an hour in something of a frozen silence. Sam smoked nonchalantly as he drove to show how much at ease he was, while inwardly he was reflecting on easy ways of chiselling Stainer out of what he thought he was going to get. And Percy?

At last Percy said, 'Fix a place where I can meet this Stainer feller. After I've talked to him I'll let you know what I think. If that doesn't suit you can include me out.'

Sam agreed that was fair enough and the conversation lapsed. When they reached Lily's pad Sam broke open a bottle of whisky from Lily's small store, and they punished it between them. Percy was out of practice after recent years of enforced abstinence, and the whisky got to him very quickly. He swore eternal brotherhood with good ol' Sammie boy, wept over the perfidy of his absconding wife, and let Sam put him to bed.

Amicable relations had been re-established, and Sam left him snorting into his messy pillow. There couldn't be any doubt now who was going to be the boss in this operation. Relieved at Lily's fortunate absence, Sam slept the sleep of the innocent.

TWO

Sam found it impossible to arrange the meeting with Stainer for a few days, so Percy borrowed the Viva one night and went to look at *'Bernie's Place'* for himself. It was technically a social club and thus not open to outsiders, but Percy paid over a pound note and was enrolled then and there as a member under a dummy name.

He bought a modest beer at an inflated

price and settled himself to give the situation his personal attention. And he had to admit that it all looked very promising.

A stand-up comic, billed as having been a sensation up at Batley and other hot spots in the North where they knew a good comic when they heard him, worked his way through his patter with some ad-libs that would not have pleased Mrs Whitehouse. A robust vocalist in a see-through gown, belted out her numbers; she was past her best, but the audience loved her. And all the while there was the happy tinkle of the cash registers.

Percy did a little discreet wandering. There was a restaurant and a noisy arena where dancing of a sort was going on, and another long bar for the serious drinkers who didn't want to be bothered with singers or strippers or kindred distractions. Every facility was being well patronised, and it was simplicity itself for Percy to amble about and get the feel of the place.

The administration precinct had plenty of doors marked *Private,* and Percy left them alone because too many staff members were moving in and out, and the last thing he wanted was to be challenged by a bouncer.

He had been listening to snippets of conversation in the long bar where the company was mostly male. He caught the punch lines of a variety of dirty jokes that didn't amuse him because he had heard them before. He was about to push off for good when he heard somebody say something about Freddie Stainer.

Then another called out, 'Hey, Freddie, come over here a minute.'

A tall young man in a midnight blue velvet jacket detached himself from the bar and saluted as he came across.

'Anything I can do, gents – at your service.' He was absorbed into the group. A glad-hander, doing his stuff with the cash customers on behalf of the management.

Long fair hair and shiny teeth, probably wearing make-up, Percy decided, and he noticed the way Stainer's gaze automatically roved about even while he appeared to be wholly taken up with his party, just in case he might be missing something. Handsome and shifty. And nothing like as sloppy as he looked.

Percy didn't hang around any more. Before he drove away he took a quick look at the rear of the main building. Part of the car park was reserved for the staff, and a door nearby was labelled: *No Admittance*. That would have to be their obvious way in, the offices would be at that end of the building.

It was not until much later that night, when Lily was finally and safely asleep alone in her bed, that Sam crept into Percy's room, and very gently closed the door. Percy had been waiting for him.

Sam wore pyjamas of a striking and unsuitably youthful blue for his unathletic frame. Percy sat on his bed in his vest and pants.

'Well, what d'you think?' Sam whispered. 'It's okay, isn't it? A gold mine, Percy.'

'I saw Stainer,' said Percy. 'I don't like working with a queer.'

'He's no poof,' said Sam. 'That's just an act he puts on, he reckons it's good for some of the trade they get in there, you know how it gets these days – he camps it up strictly for the laughs, honest. You didn't talk to him?'

'No. Just looked around. It's a possibility.'

'All that lovely lolly,' said Sam softly.

Percy got back into bed. 'I don't go too much on this Freddie Stainer, he could turn out awkward – he might be sharper than you think. I've seen his sort before, they don't con all that easy.'

Sam switched on his grin of boyish cunning. It failed to register with Percy.

'I got Freddie Stainer dangling,' said Sam. 'He's been trying to keep two birds and they come bloody expensive, Percy – the daft feller's desperate in case they find out about each other, and he's got a wife with a maintenance order out against him. I tell you, he's got more grief than he can handle, he's ready-made for a deal like the one we can offer.'

'Tell me about it in the morning,' said Percy, 'and put out the light as you go.'

Cantankerous bastard, Sam thought as he went back to his own room and climbed into bed. Anybody would think he wasn't interested. All that beefing about Freddie Stainer.

The conference took place one morning in a café in Notting Hill. Percy and Sam reached it on foot, having parked Sam's car some distance away, a precaution Percy had insisted on. Stainer was waiting for them; trade was slack and they had plenty of room to themselves. The introductions performed by Sam were minimal, and he took the chair opposite Freddie Stainer, while Percy sat off to one side like an observer.

Stainer looked tired and edgy, and he gave Percy a more than casual glance.

'I've seen you before,' he said. 'But I can't think where.'

'The long bar, two nights ago,' said Percy. 'I was looking the place over. I didn't reckon you noticed me.'

Stainer looked relieved. 'I always pride myself on my memory for faces. You should have introduced yourself, I could have shown you round the joint.'

'Would that have been smart?' said Percy. 'I saw enough on my own – so we all sit here for a little business chat.'

Sam had brought a folded newspaper. He slid it over the table towards Stainer. 'It's inside,' he said. 'Fifty.'

'Excuse me,' said Stainer. Picking up the paper he went to the back of the café and disappeared through a doorway.

'Suspicious bastard,' said Sam without rancour. A waitress arrived and they ordered coffee. Stainer returned, minus the paper, sat down and said, 'It'll do for starters. Is it on?'

'I want a sketch of the office premises,' said Percy. 'All the security details. And so forth.'

Stainer drew a long envelope out of his inside pocket.

'I'm one jump ahead of you,' he said. 'What I put inside there is worth more than five hundred to anybody who knows their stuff.'

Percy sighed softly. 'So what do we have now, an auction? Sammie, you'd better put your chum straight.'

Their coffee arrived. Sam paid. Percy made a gesture to indicate he was temporarily withdrawing from the discussion, and he was the only one to try the coffee, having had little in the way of breakfast.

'Freddie,' said Sam reproachfully, 'it's a bit

early to be jacking your price up. We got overheads to cover.'

'I know what it's worth,' said Stainer. He smiled, still holding the envelope. 'Let's hear a bid.'

Percy glanced at Sam, shrugged, and said, 'Finish your drink and we'll move off, Sam. This feller's just fooling around with us.'

'Looks that way,' said Sam. 'I thought he was smarter than that. Okay, Freddie, I'll have the fifty back.'

Stainer's confident smile slipped a little. 'A pair of cross-talk comedians. You don't bluff me, and I keep the fifty.'

'You know what you can do with our bleeding envelope,' said Sam and slurped at his coffee. 'You're a shyster and we don't want any part of you. Right, Percy?'

Percy nodded.

'Listen,' said Freddie Stainer–

–'We heard enough,' said Sam. 'You reckon you can put the bite on us, and we don't have to stand for that – it makes a bad impression on my friend here.'

'It does,' said Percy thinly.

'No hard feelings,' said Sam. 'You just kissed yourself good-bye to five centuries, Percy. I hope you can afford it.'

'It's a bluff,' said Stainer. 'You're making with the funny talk, Sam. You don't kid me.'

Sam stood up, so did Percy, and neither of them offered to shake hands with Stainer.

They left him gazing after them, and he was no longer smiling. He was puzzled and uneasy.

On the pavement outside Sam halted. 'Hang on a minute,' he said. 'It's working, watch...'

Freddie Stainer came out after them, in a hurry. He actually put his arm around Sam's shoulders.

'Hey,' he said breezily, 'what's all the rush? You blokes are a bit quick off the mark. I thought we were having a friendly discussion. Here...'

He held out the envelope. 'I'm not backing down,' he said. 'I just want to show I'm trusting you two to give me a fair deal.'

Percy slipped the envelope into his pocket. 'I'll see if it's worth the fifty Sam already gave you,' he said.

'Boy, you're a real comic,' said Stainer. 'I just handed you the full business – anybody would think I insulted you.'

They were making an untidy three-some, with Stainer in the middle, blocking the pavement.

'I put in full specifications of the safe, diagrams, the whole works,' said Stainer.

'You have to broadcast it so the flaming street can hear?' said Percy sourly, turned and walked off sharply by himself.

'He's a bit touchy,' said Stainer. 'Does he always act like that, Sam?'

31

'He's careful,' said Sam. 'He'll do a good job.'

'When?'

'Now who's rushing things?' said Sam. 'There's gear we have to collect, planning, all that – Percy doesn't believe in taking chances. We'll have another meeting in two days, same time, same place.'

'How do I get in touch with you if something comes up?' said Stainer.

'You don't,' said Sam. 'We can always find you at the club. Check?'

Stainer let it go at that. They were a cagey pair, but without him they were nothing. He was wondering if Percy was as good as Sam said he was.

It was on the following day that Lily made a remark that had some alarm bells ringing for Sam.

'You seem to be spending a lot of time with Mr Cater,' she said. 'What are you up to, Sammie?'

This was a question he could do without. Lily wasn't simple, not all that much.

'We're not up to anything,' he said. 'I just feel sorry for the poor feller, no harm in that, is there?'

They were in Lily's sitting-room. She was knitting and Sam had been scanning the newspaper. A cosy domestic scene. Percy was out looking up some of his old contacts for the gear they would need, with capital provided by Sam.

'He doesn't say much about himself, does he?' said Lily. 'Sort of secretive, wouldn't you say?'

'Oh I dunno,' said Sam. 'His wife left him while he was away from home.'

Lily made some sympathetic noises. 'No wonder he always looks so sad, and I think it's kind of you to give him so much of your time, I really do.'

'You know me,' said Sam. 'The little ray of sunshine.'

'He's out of a job, isn't he?' said Lily. 'I notice he never gets any mail. Actually I've been wondering if I was wise to let him have the room … you never can tell about people these days, but I must say he looked harmless, and after all I've got you in the house, haven't I?'

She gave Sam a tender confiding look. She was sitting curled up on the settee, showing plenty of nice rounded leg.

'I'm here all right,' said Sam. 'Don't you worry about Percy Cater. As a matter of fact, I'm thinking of putting some business his way to help him out.'

'That's kind of you,' she said, still knitting. 'Now you come to mention it, I don't know what you do for a living either, do I? You've been here weeks and weeks and I've let myself get quite fond of you, Sammie.'

Sam grinned. 'You could say I'm a general dealer, I operate by personal contact, I find what people want and the best price they'll pay – and if I'm lucky I locate the stuff, whatever it is … then I collect my commission. That's why I have to be out and about such a lot – you never know when a deal might come up.'

'I never see you doing any work here,' she said doubtfully. 'Don't you have to have an office?'

Sam tapped his forehead. 'I keep it all in here, that's my personal computer.'

'It's not like having a regular job, is it?' she said, and she had now suspended her knitting. 'I mean, if you got ill you wouldn't be earning anything, would you?'

She had the wedding bells ringing, and that tender light in her eyes warned Sam what perils might lie ahead if he didn't box it extra clever. This was no time for Lily to be showing such a close personal interest in his affairs. Once a woman got beefing about security and what about the future you could guess which way her loving mind was turning.

'Don't lose any sleep over me,' he said cheerfully. 'I'm in pretty good shape, financially – and otherwise. Do I hear a complaint, baby?'

Lily smiled and lowered her eyes modestly. 'Oh you Sam you–'

The time was right. Sam went across, took the knitting away from her, sat down beside her and scooped her legs into his lap. This would put a stop to her inconvenient cross-examination. Lily was always ready. You bet she was, and it didn't have to be in bed either.

He tilted her head and kissed her slowly and with considerable expertise, and his free roving hand began the old business with her legs.

'Now you stop it, Sam,' she murmured. 'That wasn't what I was getting at...'

'I know what I'm getting at,' he said, nibbling her ear.

Lily giggled, like a young bird being explored on a parkbench. She clung to Sam. 'You're so coarse, you really are ... oh Sam!'

'Don't talk so much,' Sam mumbled. 'Let's concentrate, baby.'

'You're a terrible greedy man,' she said, and then concentrated with the utmost willingness, to their mutual benefit.

They heard Percy return and go plodding up the stairs. They were still heavily involved and in no state to break off the engagement.

'He'll never guess what we're doing down here,' Lily whispered. Her face was flushed and she looked ten years younger. 'I do love you so, Sammie,' she said, 'or I wouldn't let you do this to me...'

'You're a knock-out,' he said with convincing ardour.

When he managed to disentangle himself
and climb into his clothes, he went up to see
how Percy had fared, and the first thing
Percy said as he entered was, 'you've been
banging that old bird again.'

'It was on offer,' said Sam. 'How could any
gentleman refuse? She's been getting too inquisitive about you and about me. It might
have been dangerous. She thinks you're a
man of mystery. I told her you had a sad
story, your wife leaving you, all that, and I
told her we might be doing some business
together–'

'You run off at the mouth too much,' said
Percy. 'In our line of business you don't tell
a woman anything. What did you tell the old
cow?'

'Nothing important,' said Sam, 'just that
we might be doing a business deal together.
That will stop her wondering why you and I
go out so often, and why I'm up here yapping with you. She's been noticing things.
So I gave her some heavy loving just now.'

'Bloody stallion,' said Percy.

Sam grinned. 'It'll keep her quiet for a bit.
How did you get on?'

'I can get most of what we need,' said Percy.
'One or two blokes I've done business with in
the past didn't want to know me any more.
The fuzz has been putting pressure on them,

36

and all these bombing jobs and terrorist threats have got some of them jittery – and the prices they were asking were crazy, bloody robbery.'

'It's a wicked world,' Sam agreed. 'You been out of circulation too long, Percy.'

'Seems like it,' said Percy gloomily. 'Soon as they hear what I want they show me the door. Bastards. I must be bad news. There's a feller over a Greenwich, Dusty Miller, he knows me from the old days, and he didn't throw a fit when he heard it was me on the blower. He's got the oxyacetylene gear I want, and he won't rob us. We can pick it up tonight.'

'You want me with you?' said Sam.

'That stuff comes heavy,' said Percy wearily. 'I'm not trying to lug a cylinder about on my own, and you might as well start getting your hands dirty. You might also like to be there and see I'm not gypping you – Dusty won't be giving the gear away, you know, so make sure you have your wallet handy. You can chalk it all up to working expenses.'

'I intend to do just that,' said Sam.

That night they drove across to Greenwich. Dusty Miller had a small workshop in a dingy street not far from the river. There was a double door leading into a yard. Percy hammered on it and presently Dusty opened up and they drove inside, and the doors were shut behind them. There were no lights visible, and the place looked derelict.

Dusty Miller was a disembodied voice in the dark. 'Who's the bloke with you, Percy?'

'He's okay,' said Percy. 'He's my partner.'

Dusty led them in through a doorway and shut the door before turning on the light. He was a small bald man with bushy eyebrows and a heavy square face; a deliberate and slow-moving man in a stained brown suit.

They were in a small office and through the glass panels they could see into the adjoining workshop, and the shadowy shapes of a variety of vehicles, none of them clearly fit for the road; there was a smell of oil and metal and old rubber.

Dusty indicated the gear under a bench by the door into the workshop.

'It's all there,' he said. 'I have to have it back, Percy.'

'You'll get it back and in good order,' said Percy.

'Doing without it will cost me money,' said Dusty. 'It's the only cutting gear I got, how long will you want it for?'

'Three or four days,' said Percy. 'A week at the outside.'

He stooped and began to inspect the apparatus, while Dusty Miller propped himself against the wall.

'I'm doing you a favour, Percy,' he said. 'I hear you've been out of luck lately.'

Percy straightened up and wiped his hands on the seat of his trousers.

'Don't talk to me about luck,' he said.

'I wouldn't want any of that traced back to me,' said Dusty. 'I'll be frank with you, Percy – it wouldn't worry me if you took your business somewhere else–'

'But you'll still do me a favour,' said Percy.

'For a pal,' said Dusty.

'How much?' said Sam, who felt it was time he got into the dialogue.

'For a week,' said Dusty. 'Fifty.'

'Some pal,' said Sam. 'We're not offering to buy the stuff, we only want to hire it.'

'I take the risk,' said Dusty. 'Listen, as soon as a job gets pulled the fuzz are in and out of places like mine all the time, messing us about, turning everything over...'

'You're breaking my heart,' said Sam. 'I reckon thirty will be plenty.'

'No deal,' said Dusty.

'Let's go back to the other bloke, Percy,' said Sam. 'He'll settle for thirty.'

'That's an old gag,' said Dusty. 'You don't have anybody else lined up.'

Sam had taken his wallet out, he had been tapping it on his hand. Now he put it back with a gesture of disgust, and he made sure Dusty was watching.

Percy shook his head at Dusty. 'You surprise me, I didn't expect this from you, Dusty.'

'Everything's gone up,' said Dusty. 'How long you been away, Percy?'

'Too long for some people,' said Percy.

'Come on, Percy,' said Sam. 'We're wasting time here. I never did fancy being taken to the cleaners, even if he is an old mate of yours.'

'Listen,' said Dusty, 'I tell you what we'll do – we'll split the difference, how's that? That's a fair offer. It's all yours for forty. You won't do better than that anywhere else … these are very dicey times, Percy, I have to protect myself, and I got the business here to think of.'

Sam gazed around the littered workshop. 'That shouldn't take long, I'd set fire to it if I were you. I'll give you thirty-five, cash now.'

'I'm robbing myself,' said Dusty.

'You should live that long,' said Sam and took out his wallet again. Dusty watched him count out the money in fives, and he noted, as Sam had intended he should, that thirty-five didn't leave Sam's wallet empty.

'We might be doing some business together some time,' said Sam, with the air of a man with large resources and limitless opportunities. 'This is just peanuts, Dusty, I know – a few quid for the loan of some gear. I'm thinking of the real money, know what I

40

mean? I hear you're pretty smart doctoring a car for a quick sale, but you have to be doing it in a big way if you want to get anywhere – do I take you with me? There's the question of financing – to operate properly you might need some backing ... one of these days we'll have to have a little chat.'

Dusty Miller nodded, a little out of his depth.

'Thirty-five for a start,' said Sam, smiling.

Dusty took the money. 'With a partner like you,' he said, 'I could put my feet up and retire. Where did you find him, Percy?'

'Buckingham Palace, where else?' said Percy with his customary sourness. 'Let's get this gear loaded.'

Sam drove back with extra caution, because the contents of the Viva's boot together with Percy's recent record would make things very awkward if a patrol had any excuse to stop and check them. So whenever a Panda car appeared in their vicinity Sam was probably the most punctilious driver in the metropolis.

And because of the number of light-fingered bastards about, Sam agreed it would be unwise to follow his normal practice and leave the car in the street. They put it in an all-night park where there was a proper attendant on duty, and completed their journey by bus.

The second meeting with Freddie Stainer was rather more cordial than the first, so much so that eventually they adjourned to a pub where the atmosphere was more relaxed, and since it was middle morning they got a corner of the lounge bar to themselves, where they got down to the serious details.

THREE

Percy was in charge. The safe was a Waterson *Supremo,* set in reinforced concrete in a small strong-room that was itself protected by a steel door to which only the manager and the bank held keys; and the whole business had an electronic alarm connected to the neighbouring police station.

Stainer would see that the alarm was neutralised on the night they went in.

'It ought to be tomorrow night,' he said. 'There's a one-night booking that'll pack them in solid – Big Happy Bossic, his first appearance in this country–'

'Never heard of him,' said Percy.

'He's a hot property,' said Stainer. 'He drives 'em crazy, it could be the biggest rave-up since we opened – we'll gross four thousand, sure to.'

'Won't that mean they'll lay on extra security?' said Sam. 'Flocks of coppers?'

'Maybe,' said Stainer. 'But Big Happy never performs anywhere after midnight, he has it written into his contract, some kind of a private kink ... anyway, as soon as it's midnight he's off stage and that's your lot.'

'Cinderella,' said Sam.

'It's part of his gimmick,' said Stainer. 'He's weird all right, but it pays off, and the place will go dead after he finishes, the boss hasn't even bothered to book anybody else – nobody with any reputation wants to follow Big Happy Bossic from Nashville. The police will be off the scene and by one o'clock we'll be shut tight.'

'I'll need three hours,' said Percy. 'What about police patrols? We can't have a car standing there at the rear while we're inside.'

'There's an enclosure by the kitchen, where they line up the dust bins and stuff,' said Stainer. 'If you drive your car in there it can't be seen from the road.' He pushed an envelope across the table to Percy. 'I had a key copied, it'll get you into the kitchen, and before I go off duty tomorrow night I undertake to see that the alarm isn't operating. I can't do any more than that.'

'Fix yourself a cast-iron alibi,' said Sam. 'The fuzz will start by leaning on all you boys who work there.'

'I'll take care of that,' said Stainer.

And it won't be your wife, Sam was thinking.

'There's one thing we haven't fixed,' said Stainer.

'Afterwards?' said Sam, very soberly. 'Like where we meet so you can collect your slice? Right?'

'It's a good point,' said Percy. 'What do you have in mind, Freddie?'

'I could call at your place,' said Stainer.

'There's a car park behind this pub,' said Sam. 'We'll be waiting for you the next morning, about eleven.'

'That means you don't trust me, and you expect me to trust you,' said Stainer. 'I don't even know where I can get in touch with you two. Looks like a lousy arrangement to me.'

'I never mix my private life with my business,' said Percy.

Freddie made a snorting noise to indicate what he thought of that. And Percy gave him a very cold eye.

'Let's have it,' he said. 'You think we'll pull the job and scarper.'

'I never said that,' Stainer protested.

'If you think that we'll forget it here and now,' said Percy. 'That's not the way I operate, Mister Bleeding Stainer.'

'Listen, sport,' said Sam, 'we're the ones who'll be doing the trusting, me and Percy – we'll be trusting you to snaffle that alarm, and if you fall down on that little job we won't know a thing until the fuzz arrives to collect us, so let's have no more of that crap about who trusts who. It has to be mutual, or we call it off now.'

'We had this scene before,' said Percy. 'I always worked on my own before. I never had to trust anybody but myself, and listening to you, Freddie, only shows how right I was. Sam was right – it's mutual or it's nothing.'

'We've got all the apparatus to get through to that safe,' said Sam. 'There isn't a better bloke in the business than Percy here, but we'll let you have the gear for what we paid for it, and you can find yourself another pair of partners – maybe we'll be reading about it in the papers. Chew it over, boyo, while I get us some more drinks.'

He went over to the bar and chatted to the barman while he poured whisky for the three of them. There was a bowl of peanuts on the bar. Sam helped himself liberally and didn't hurry back to the discussion. They had Freddie Stainer wobbling, and Percy had that insulted look on his miserable face – his integrity had been questioned, and by a flaming amateur at that.

Sam let the atmosphere build up. They were talking and Freddie was the eager one now, putting over some point. When Sam strolled back with the drinks he didn't take his seat, to show that he expected it was all over.

'Mud in your eye,' he said. 'Are we moving, Percy?'

Percy grunted and pointed to the chair, and Sam sat.

'What's the score now?' he said.

'We made a friendly agreement,' said Percy, and sounded anything but friendly. 'A little adjustment in Freddie's slice, anything over three and a half thousand he gets, on top of the five.'

'Nice for Freddie,' said Sam, and smiled as he added: 'there'll be no fiddling because Freddie will see to it that he's in the office when they count it.'

'Check,' said Freddie. 'You wouldn't expect anything else, would you? Normal business practice. Eleven o'clock here, the morning after.'

The conference broke up shortly afterwards, and as Percy left with Sam he made the obvious comment: 'he's a suspicious bastard, Sammie.'

'Aren't we all?' said Sam, and grinned to take the sting out of it.

'We'll take a look at the target in daylight,' said Percy. 'I never like going into a job cold, I like to know all about my surroundings before I start – that seem fussy to you?'

Sam agreed it didn't. He also needed a final check on the roads they would be using, because it would never do to discover at the last minute that a road had been dug up and closed to traffic in the area that would matter to them.

Bearing in mind what was in the boot, Sam drove sedately. They parked behind one of the super-markets, and proceeded on foot. Outside *'Bernie's Place'* they joined a group of fans who were gazing at the garish posters almost in a hushed reverence. Big Happy Bossic was billed as the one and only super-sensational smash-hit, in his first and only appearance in the UK.

There was a series of blown-up pictures, illustrating Big Happy in various agonised attitudes in sequined pants and not much else – a muscular and hairy man, shining with sweat and making sad noises with a guitar.

It was to be a ticket-only performance, and there was a queue at the box office.

They wandered around the side of the building. It had originally been a cinema, and extensions had been added at the rear for the restaurant and the dance floor, and the office accommodation. They saw the enclosed space Freddie Stainer had mentioned; from a brewer's truck supplies for the bars were being taken in, and two other vans were being unloaded. They found it a busy and

47

encouraging scene.

'Tomorrow night,' said Sam. 'Wham-bang for good old Big Happy!'

They walked about some more, following up the side roads that would enable Sam to drive each way without having to use the main roads. They even walked past the local nick, and found it just a shade too near *'Bernie's Place'*. They saw a squad car being washed in the yard, and another nosed out into the road just in front of them.

Percy said nothing, just gave Sam one of his melancholy looks.

'I knew a bloke once,' said Sam cheerfully. 'He busted into this place and lifted a lot of lovely gear and got clean away. He nearly had a fit when he read in the papers and found he'd done the Chief Constable's pad.'

'Didn't do his home work,' said Percy, as sour as ever.

'He still got the loot,' said Sam.

'He should have got nicked,' said Percy. 'That's no way to work.'

They ended their exploration back in the shopping area, Sam reckoned he could find his way around in a hurry and with both eyes shut. He was hungry, while Percy appeared able to do without food when his mind was on a job. Sam won and they found a café and some moderate nosh.

'What about this old bird of yours?' said Percy. 'We'll both be out tomorrow night, we don't want her getting nosy.'

'I already prepared the ground,' said Sam. 'I told her we'd be taking a trip together soon, a business trip up to Brum... I'm introducing you to some of my contacts. She thinks it's very kind of me to take such an interest in a lonely feller like you.'

'What about afterwards?' said Percy. 'If you stay there she'll get her hooks into you, Sammie. I tell you that for free. She's soft on you and she might reckon you're her last chance, and you'll have a bit of spending money.'

Sam grinned. 'I like the spending money bit. You can forget the rest. I got it all taped. I don't mind giving her a bit of a bundle when I'm in the mood – and to tell you the truth, Percy, I've had many a worse lay in my time; maybe she's no chicken, but she's still in good working order – but there's nothing permanent in it for me. Hell no.'

'Watch your step,' said Percy. 'She's at the dangerous age.'

'I play it by my own rules,' said Sam placidly. 'Always have done, always will. Come to that, Percy, I wouldn't say you're the right bloke to give me any advice about how to handle a woman.'

'You're a right little louse,' said Percy. 'You make use of everybody you come across, and that includes me.'

'What I like about you, Percy,' said Sam, 'you're as good as a tonic, so what are you beefing about now? I did the research, I made the contact – and I've been finding the finance. Where would you be without me?'

Percy went on digging at his eggs and chips, the best the café could raise at the end of the lunch period.

'Come on, Percy,' said Sam. 'Give us a smile.'

'Up yours,' said Percy. 'We pull this job, then we split.'

Sam nodded. 'Just what I planned myself. All clean and tidy. Anything else on your mind?'

'Stainer,' said Percy. 'I've never had to rely on a bloke like him before, he's too much of an amateur.'

'I wouldn't choose him myself,' Sam agreed, 'but he's getting plenty out of this, Percy, and he's in a mess for money – he can't afford to have it fall down.'

'They'll know it's an inside job soon as they look at it,' said Percy.

'That's Freddie's headache,' said Sam.

'They'll put them all through the wringer,' said Percy, 'from the manager downwards. Is Stainer so dumb he doesn't know that?'

'He's dumb,' said Sam.

When Sam told Lily he would definitely be away with Percy Cater for a night, she said that if she didn't know him better she might have thought he had another woman tucked away somewhere. She said it with such an arch smile that both of them knew she didn't mean it seriously, but needed reassuring.

In the course of that night Sam gave her ample proof that she was indeed all any healthy man could desire, and they killed most of a bottle of gin in the process. Sam had the private feeling that this might well be his farewell performance, so it had to be a good one. Once he got his slice of the loot it would be safer to be off and away, because it was now very clear that Lily had the starlight in her loving eyes, portending a cosy future for them together.

She was starting to take a wifely interest in Sam's clothes, and his general health and welfare. He had to promise not to drink and smoke too much while he was away, and to drive very carefully.

It was murder on Sam's nerves, and reinforced his decision to give her the old heaveho without delay. She said she might visit her sister in Kingston while Sam was away.

'I don't like stopping here alone now at night,' she said. 'Not without you to look after me, Sammie – it never used to worry me, but it does now.'

She was being the helpless little woman,

clinging to her protector, which was something of a new role for Sam Harris, and one he could have done without.

To sustain the fiction of the trip to Birmingham they had to leave the house early in the afternoon, each with luggage for the night. Sam had a suit-case, in which he had prudently packed his best gear, since it was no part of their plan to return to Lily's domicile afterwards. They arranged their departure to coincide with Lily's absence shopping, otherwise she might have wanted to know why Sam needed such a big case for one night. Everything Percy owned that was worth salvaging went into one small case.

They had hours to put in somehow, and Sam refused to drive around aimlessly. That stuff in the boot made him jittery. Suppose some clot hit them in the rear and smashed the boot and a copper arrived to sort it out? It happens all the time in the traffic. Ask anybody. Too risky, and not necessary.

They left the car in the same park as before, they could collect it any time. They took several bus rides, and ran out of conversation. Sam was quite ready to pass the time on his own, without Percy trailing after him, but Percy wouldn't wear that.

'We stick together, Sammie boy,' he said. 'I want you where I can see you – you might fall over and break a leg, you might slide under a bus, you might get mugged even – this is a wicked city.'

They passed some hours in a cinema. It was a sex film with lots of rude nudes. Percy went to sleep, and Sam learnt nothing that wasn't already in his repertoire. They had a late leisurely supper, with nothing liquid but coffee: Percy didn't drink when he had a job on hand, and he didn't allow Sam the chance to do otherwise, which made the meal a little less than festive.

Sam was chain-smoking and couldn't leave his watch alone. There was no visible change in Percy's demeanour. He just looked tired, and acted as though he had nothing ahead of him but the prospect of a good night's sleep.

Zero hour. A few minutes after two in the morning, Sam was steering the Viva quietly across the parking place behind the club. It was a clear starlit night and he needed no lights now. The gate leading to the enclosure by the kitchen had been padlocked, and Sam sat in the car while Percy worked on the padlock. It took a matter of seconds, and then Sam drove in and parked just clear of the line of dust bins.

They unloaded the boot and carried the gear across to the kitchen door, where Percy used the key Freddie Stainer had provided. The oxyacetylene cylinder was awkward and it took the pair of them to carry it.

They closed the kitchen door, but left it unlocked because it was their exit route, and they would not want to dawdle over their departure. They humped their stuff along a corridor past the kitchen and across a space with a rubber-tiled floor and plenty of doors. They knew the door they wanted, into the manager's office. It was locked, and Percy whistled softly while he worked over it and Sam held the torch and smoked two quick cigarettes. Percy had made him wear rubber gloves, and he didn't handle his cigarettes too cleverly. So Percy told him to pack it in and attend to their business, and Percy was now demonstrably the boss.

They got into the office with little trouble. It was an inside room with no windows, so it was safe to use the lights. The miniature strong-room was behind some imitation panelling, where Stainer's sketch had indicated.

Percy slid the panelling aside, drew up a chair and sat to examine the steel door. And Sam had a sudden icy feeling down his back: if Freddie Stainer had fallen down on the job the alarm bells would be ringing in the police station, and any minute now Panda cars would converge on *'Bernie's Place'*.

Percy didn't share his nervousness, he was too busy. He had given the door a minute inspection, tapping it gently here and there, always whistling softly like any workman, and ignoring Sam absolutely. He connected the cutting apparatus to the cylinder and put on his goggles.

'How long do you reckon it'll take, Percy?' said Sam.

Percy grunted. The white flame was hissing and spitting. He squatted and applied it to the door, and there was no other sound in the room but the roar of the flame cutting into the metal.

Sam relaxed. Freddie Stainer had done his stuff on the alarm. Sam nosed around the manager's desk. Business correspondence didn't interest him. There was no cash anywhere that he looked. No liquor. He found some cigars and a girlie calendar that was not fit for public display.

The minutes dragged along. It was no use asking Percy how he was managing because he didn't answer, but Sam could see part of the circular groove he was cutting in the door.

After a while Sam's bladder was calling urgently for attention. The effect of his panic, perhaps, or the gallons of coffee he had swilled down. He looked for the manager's toilet, he found a door that should have been the right one because it had *Cloakroom* on it, but it was locked.

'Just going to spring a leak, Percy,' Sam called out. 'Won't be long. Okay?' Percy didn't even turn his head from the job.

Taking the torch, Sam went back into the kitchen area, and found a staff toilet. Afterwards he drifted about and came across the place where the crates were stacked – the empties. Every other door he tried was locked, and he had brought nothing with him to coax them open.

They had already been in there damn nearly an hour, and it seemed longer than that to Sam. In his time he had fiddled his way into places where he had no right to be – a hotel room, for instance, while nobody was around – but he had always been after a quick scoop of what might be available, and then out again.

This was different. He was just a spectator, and he was finding it hard on the nerves.

He went back, and he might never have been away for all the notice Percy took. He could sit at the desk and play a game of Patience, if he could find a deck of cards.

When he asked Percy if there was anything he could do, Percy told him to keep out of the bleeding way because he had nearly finished.

The circular hole in the door had been completed and the circle of cut metal was ready to be lifted out to disclose the aperture. Parts of the metal were still hot, and Percy used a thin pair of pincers with long handles. His face was streaked with sweat, and he was frowning intently as he reached inside the hole he had made.

He squirmed and groped and muttered to himself, and when he withdrew his hand the door began to swing open, and a light went on in the small strong-room.

Percy glanced at Sam. 'How about that then?' he said.

'Very nice,' said Sam.

'Bleeding perfect so far.' Percy squatted in front of the tall safe. 'This bastard might take a bit of blowing. Sammie, you get all the rugs you can find, bits of carpet, anything that'll quieten her down when she goes off.'

It took Percy nearly half an hour before he was satisfied with the explosives he had packed around the hinges of the safe. Sam had collected a couple of thick rugs and a strip of carpet and some cushions. They piled them up close against the front of the safe and wedged a chair in to hold the bundle tight.

Percy trailed the wires out through the hole in the door and closed the door. He followed Sam along the wall. He wiped his mouth.

'Haven't done any of this for a while,' he said. 'Might blow it all through the flaming roof, you never can tell. It's tricky stuff.'

Sam watched him nervously. He had never handled explosives himself, and he was hoping Percy hadn't forgotten too much of his old skill.

'No good hanging around,' said Percy. 'Stand by for blasting.'

He completed the circuit. There were two muffled booms in rapid succession. The floor seemed to lift a little under their feet, and the steel door flew open.

Percy exhaled noisily and almost smiled. The overhead light in the strong-room had gone, and they could see the thin fumes of the explosion drifting out, and the scorched fragments of fabric blown from the front of the safe. The air inside was hot and acrid.

Sam wanted to start, but Percy held him back. 'Have to let it settle in there,' he said.

Sam was tense. 'That sounded bloody loud to me,' he whispered. 'Suppose somebody heard, Percy?'

'That's a chance we take,' said Percy. 'Who's going to be around here at close on four in the morning?'

'Coppers,' said Sam.

Percy made a disgusted sound. 'They drive around in cars, boy, they don't pound a beat, not any more. Get a grip on yourself before you wet your pants. This is the last time I'll ever have you out on a job, you're too flaming jittery.'

Sam just glared at him angrily, unable to share his composure and remembering how the floor had jumped under his feet. There might be some inconvenient bastard on the phone to the fuzz, while they stood around like a pair of whores at a christening.

'Okay,' said Percy at length. 'Let's see what we did for ourselves.'

He had the torch and Sam carried the bag they expected to fill.

FOUR

By the light of Percy's torch they saw a satisfactory sight. The door of the safe had been blown off its hinges and hung out at an angle wide enough for Percy to reach inside. Some of the stacked money had been disturbed by the blast and lay scattered around. There were three deep shelves, and they appeared to be nicely loaded with currency. The space at the top was occupied by accounts books, probably the ones the Inland Revenue never saw.

'Boy,' said Sam reverently, and began to collect up the scattered notes from the floor. It was a beautiful feeling, to squat surrounded by money.

Percy was handing him back neat packets of fifties and hundreds in used notes, and they were soon well over the three thousand mark, and the bag was bulging. On the very lowest shelf there were little bags of fifty-pence pieces, a hundred in each, plus bags of ten-pence pieces and stacks of coppers.

'What a bleeding shame we don't have room for all of it,' said Percy. 'We should've brought a barrow.'

Sam was stuffing the cash in, and he was actually having to discard pound notes to make room for the packets of new fivers that Percy had liberated. Fivers with the bank wrappers still on them, staff salaries, no doubt.

'Can't take much more,' he said.

'Find some paper bags,' Percy snapped. 'Let's do a proper job on it now we're here ... wrap 'em in newspapers, stuff your pockets – use your loaf, for Gawd's sake, Sam!'

He slung out the bags of fifty pence pieces, there were six of them in all, and Sam carried them out of the way and put them on the desk. He looked in vain for paper bags, or any other suitable containers. The best he could do was a box file with papers inside. He chucked the papers on the floor and rejoined the scene.

Percy was ramming bundles of notes into his pockets. Sam knelt and did the same, opting automatically for the tidy packets of fivers. There was no sound but the pleasant rustle of money. Loose notes he put inside his shirt, scooping them up in handfuls.

'Now I know what they mean when they say a feller's loaded, Percy,' he said happily.

'Must be near five thousand,' said Percy. 'We'll skip the small silver and the coppers.' He had clicked the lock on the bag with some difficulty. 'Over two thousand clear, each.'

Sam grinned. 'Too bad about Freddie Stainer, right?'

'Very sad,' said Percy flatly. 'He'll know better next time.'

'You bet he will,' said a new voice out in the office. 'Come on out where I can see you, you pair of lousy twisters.'

Freddie Stainer stood by the desk with his hands behind his back; he still wore dress trousers and a bow tie, but a tweed jacket in place of his dinner jacket. And he was not smiling.

'I heard all that,' he said.

'Now listen, Freddie,' said Sam. 'You got it all wrong–'

'No,' said Stainer. 'I heard enough. So I don't get anything. You made a nice big haul and so you're going to scarper and I'm to be the mug–'

'It wasn't like that,' said Sam earnestly. 'You must have misunderstood, Freddie, we wouldn't do that to you.'

'Too bloody right you won't,' said Stainer. 'That's why I'm here. I've been here all along.'

Sam glanced at the cloakroom door.

'That's right,' said Stainer. 'It was worth

the wait.'

'So you never left the building,' said Sam.

'I didn't trust you two,' said Stainer, 'and how right I was.'

'You know what you've done,' said Percy, 'you've busted your alibi.'

'Not a chance,' said Stainer. 'She'll swear I was with her all night.' He gave them his glad-handed greeter's smile. 'So you pulled the job under my personal supervision, as you might say.'

Percy was holding the bag still. 'Well there's only one suggestion I can make – we do a three-way split here and now.'

'No split,' said Stainer.

'You mean you're going to turn us over to the fuzz?' said Sam. 'Is that what you're getting at? You reckon you'll pick up a reward from the firm? And you'd shop two mates for that and all over a little misunderstanding? Freddie boy, that's no way to carry on–'

'Don't come any nearer,' said Stainer. He brought his right hand round and showed them the gun.

Sam halted. This wasn't funny any more. He glanced back at Percy and Percy wasn't laughing either.

'Don't be daft, Freddie,' Sam said. 'You know you'd never use it.'

'No?' said Stainer, and smiled wider than ever as he thumbed the safety catch off. 'Try me, Sammie boy.'

'You want to watch what you're doing with that thing,' said Percy, and for a man who could handle explosives so competently he sounded very nervous.

'I could get the both of you,' said Stainer, 'then I'd be a hero, think of it that way – I surprised you robbing the safe, you both came at me, so I had to let you have it. Self-defence.'

'I believe he would at that,' said Sam to Percy. 'Okay, Freddie, what's the deal? You got us by the short and curlies. You know you'd never get away with that self-defence yarn, it's too full of holes – like how you just came to be here with a gun, for which I bet you don't happen to have a permit, so I wouldn't try that one if I were you. What's wrong with a nice friendly share-out here? Show him, Percy.'

'Don't bother,' said Stainer. 'I know what we took in last night.'

'Well then,' said Sam persuasively, 'you know there's enough for all of us.'

'Correction,' said Stainer. 'I'm taking it all. Didn't you mugs guess that? That's what this is all about.'

Percy had been quiet and still for a while. Now he ducked his head and clutched the bag to his chest and stared at the carpet.

'That's a lousy idea,' he said. 'I do the work and I don't get anything? Sam, this mate of yours is crazy–'

'I'm the smartest one here,' said Stainer. 'You thought you'd gyp me out of my cut, but it didn't work – I scoop the lot, that's fair enough–'

'Freddie,' said Sam, 'you're not being reasonable...'

'Put that bag on the floor and empty your pockets, both of you,' said Stainer, 'then get the hell out of here.' He waved the gun around between the two targets. 'Come on, you mugs, I've been standing here long enough.'

Percy and Sam exchanged glances, and there was little comfort between them. This was disaster. Sam's natural resilience prompted him to make one more attempt.

'You take half, Freddie,' he said coaxingly, 'then we'll all be happy–'

'You've got a nerve,' said Stainer. 'I don't have to bargain with you. I take the lot, now – so give and let's have no more chat.'

'I bet that gun's a dummy,' said Sam. 'You wouldn't have the guts for the real thing.'

As though some hidden spring inside him had suddenly uncoiled, Percy began to run for the door. He still held the loaded bag high against his chest, which did nothing to increase his speed, and he was not naturally an athletic performer. Yet he might have reached the door if his own clumsiness hadn't sent him stumbling against the desk on the way.

'No!' Sam shouted as he saw Stainer turn

and point the gun. 'Don't!'

Stainer had his face screwed up, as though scared of the noise the gun might make, and he didn't seem to be looking at Percy as he fired. The explosion filled the room.

Percy slid along the front of the desk and fell on his face, quite gently, and the bag rolled free on the carpet.

'You stupid bastard!' Sam whispered. 'You didn't have to do that—'

Stainer's face was ashen. 'I didn't aim at him – you saw me, Sam – I didn't mean to hit him – I honestly didn't mean it to happen–'

'Who pulled the bloody trigger?' said Sam grimly.

Percy's shoulders twitched. He got up on one elbow, blood gushed from his mouth, and he sank back.

'He shouldn't have tried to run,' said Stainer rapidly. 'Listen, Sam – it was his own fault ... he should have stopped, I wasn't even aiming at him – I only wanted to frighten him ... you saw it happen, Sam – I swear I didn't try to hit him...' Stainer was babbling in his anxiety to convince Sam it had been nothing more than a little accident. 'He'll be all right ... won't he?' His voice tailed off.

Sam knelt by the body. He didn't touch it. Percy's sad old face was twisted sideways on the carpet, and his eyes were closed. The bullet had got him in the back, almost between the shoulder blades.

'Percy,' Sam whispered. 'Can you hear me... Percy? Say something ... Percy...'

There was no movement, just a faint tremor in the gaping lips where the blood oozed.

Sam got up. 'He's still alive – I'm going to phone for an ambulance–'

As he moved to the phone on the desk, Stainer shoved himself in the way and slammed his hand on the phone.

'No,' he said, 'you can't do that, that'll get us all into trouble, Sam–'

'I'm not leaving him here,' said Sam.

'Think a minute,' said Stainer. 'What good will it do? He's as good as dead, you can see that. Listen to me, Sam. Let's just take the cash and get out of here, you and me – why stick your neck out for a dead man? Where's the sense in that? It's bloody daft, isn't it? Look at him, Sam – he won't last ten minutes...'

Stainer still had one hand down hard on the phone, and the other held the gun, and now he was lifting it to point at Sam's chest just a few inches away, and there was that crazy look in his eyes, and Sam knew that if he didn't do something smart and fast he'd end up down there with Percy.

'What's it going to be, Sam?' said Stainer. 'You with me or not? Hurry–'

'Don't have much choice, do I?' said Sam. He had been groping behind him on the desk, and his fist had fastened on one of those bags of fifty pence pieces.

Stainer nodded. 'I'm giving you a chance–'

'Is he really dead?' said Sam.

And Stainer did just what Sam had been hoping for. He turned his head to glance down. Sam chopped down on the gun and swung the bag forward and over his shoulder to hit Stainer on the side of his face so that he staggered back and dropped the gun and bent over with his face covered in his hands.

Sam had felt the impact right up his arm. It had been a very satisfactory overarm smash, and with a little more luck it would have put Stainer down for a while. He was weaving around, his sight had been blurred, and he couldn't locate the gun.

'God, I'll kill you for that … you dirty little twister…' His voice was thick and strangulated. But he was getting his bearings now.

Sam realised he had waited too long. Stainer was between him and the door. So Sam tried another swing with that lethal little bag of coins, and if it had landed it would have put Stainer away for a long time. But it missed, Stainer ducked under it, and Sam fell sprawling under his own impetus, and the bag swung across the room against the wall.

He could see the gun, it was just out of his reach, and now it was his only hope – Stainer was younger and bigger and stronger, he wasn't lying on the floor either, and he had seen the gun. They both darted for it, and Sam lost by a couple of inches and saw Stainer kick the gun clear across the room.

'Now I'm gonna tear your head off,' Stainer grunted and lifted his foot. Sam was on his knees. He grabbed Stainer's other leg and heaved with everything he had left in him, and Stainer came down heavily on his back.

It was a lucky throw and Sam knew he couldn't hope to repeat it. He couldn't see the gun and without it he would be taken apart. Already Stainer was sitting up and shaking his bemused head. Sam scrambled to his feet and made for the door. He slammed it behind him and he was in the dark corridor, stumbling for the way out and bumping into things he didn't remember seeing when they came in, bits of awkward furniture and wooden containers, and when he found himself floundering noisily among the crates of empties he had the good sense to chuck some of them behind him in case Stainer came after him.

He was panting when he got to the kitchen and his legs were shaky. He tugged the door open and more or less fell out into the fresh air – and it smelt just beautiful.

68

This was Sam Harris on the run again, and with the best of good reasons. Survival. And maybe a bloke after him with a gun.

He scuttled madly across the open space to the enclosure where the car stood. He hadn't locked it and he had the ignition key ready as soon as he tumbled himself inside. The engine caught nicely and he reversed fast out past the line of dust bins and he didn't hit one of them. No lights on yet.

The reversing was a shade too fierce, and he had to stamp on the brakes to avoid the wall behind. Then he stalled his engine like any novice, and when he shifted about in obscene fury all the notes inside his shirt crackled, and the pockets of his trousers were tight with their packets of fivers.

He made himself pause for a couple of deep breaths, and got into bottom gear without any more panic. He pulled at the wheel to straighten the car, and Freddie Stainer lurched out of the darkness and grabbed at the door on Sam's side.

'Sammie, Sammie – for God's sake, wait for me!' He was holding on to the top of the door with one hand, his elbow over, and his face was a white blur with the moving darkness of his mouth.

Sam punched at the face so close to him and Stainer's teeth cut his knuckles, but he still held on, and Sam got a glimpse of the bag in Stainer's hand. He accelerated violently and swung the car right and left and right again. There was a high-pitched scream, Stainer's face dropped out of sight, and then his arm let go. Sam felt the soft bump under his rear wheel, switched on his lights, and drove across the tarmac to the exit and out into the road, and he didn't look back.

Stainer must have taken a bump when he got shaken off. The thought didn't bother Sam much, or the recollection that Stainer had brought that loaded bag with him, because he probably had got the gun in his pocket and if Sam had stopped to pick him up, Stainer wouldn't have parted with any of the loot – he would have clobbered Sam on some quiet piece of road and then taken off with all of it. That was the kind of untrustworthy bloke Freddie Stainer was.

Imagine hiding in the gents all the time while they did the work, and then thinking he could pop out with his little gun and grab it all! What a lousy attitude.

Percy was different. What Sam had left in the way of a conscience was stirring, slowly, but enough to have him stopping at a phone box. He dialled Police and snapped it at them straight – a robbery and a shooting at *'Bernie's Place'* – they would need an ambulance – they started the usual business about who was calling, but Sam had gone.

Maybe Percy wasn't as bad as he looked. At least Sam had done the decent thing, he felt. If he'd hung around that office Stainer would have plugged him as well, and what good would that have done old Percy?

The top priority now was to get as far from the area as he could and as fast as he could. The fuzz might be swarming around there pretty soon. They might even be in time to grab Freddie Stainer. He must have been bruised and there had been no sign of a car parked anywhere near *'Bernie's Place'*, so Stainer wouldn't get very far, and he'd have the bag with him ... let him laugh himself out of that one.

Nobody else had touched that gun, only Stainer. If Percy was dead, then Stainer was in a real mess all right.

He would sing to the fuzz loud and clear, sure he would. He'd give them Sam's name, but he couldn't give them an address, and he had never seen Sam's car in daylight.

All the same, there were some angles to be considered. The roads up to London would be the first to be checked and maybe blocked. They'd expect Sam to bolt for cover and London would be the obvious place, and Stainer knew he was a Londoner.

Sam took the first road south that he came to. It was nearly five in the morning, and that was a hell of a time to be looking for cover in a hurry. He met very little traffic, almost no private cars, just goods lorries and so forth.

He switched to a secondary road, heading

out into the country and well off the London route. Now he had the time to realise that he wasn't sitting comfortably because of all the cash stuffed about him, especially inside his shirt. This was the first time in his life that he had found money any kind of an irritation.

He pulled in and stopped at a field gate miles from anywhere. He fished out the crumpled notes from inside his shirt, there wasn't time to count them, but they made a sizeable bundle. He reached back for that case he had so providentially brought with him, and the cash went in under his clothes.

Counting what he had stuffed into the pockets of his jacket and trousers was easy: six neat packets of fivers, a hundred quid a time.

Not bad, Sammie boy, he told himself. It could have been more, but then it could have been a damn sight worse if he'd let Freddie Stainer take over, and it was all clear profit.

He reckoned he must be worth over nine hundred quid as he sat there, counting what he'd carried with him at the start. And he was at liberty, that was the big thing. It was rough on old Percy – now there was a feller with bad luck around his neck.

With everything now stowed away, Sam resumed his journey. After that very active and crowded night he should have been short of sleep, but he felt wide awake and as sharp as ever. He had run out of cigarettes and he could do with some grub pretty soon. Otherwise everything was under control and the outlook was fine and rosy. *'Bernie's Place'* was already some forty safe miles behind him, and London even further.

He was meeting a little more traffic now, but he hadn't seen a single squad car yet. There had been some tricky moments back there at that place, but he had got away with it. What he had to do now was find a place to dig himself in and let it all quieten down. Stainer could squeal all he liked, but Sam Harris wasn't going to let that throw him into a panic.

It was years since he had been a customer of the police, and they had no recent addresses to connect with him. They'd do their routine checking in London for a start, and it wouldn't get them much.

It was then he thought of Lily. And his empty stomach turned right over. That bastard Stainer would surely give the fuzz the name of Sam Harris, they would print it in the papers, and Lily would see it, and she knew what kind of car he had – hell, he had even let her drive it on a couple of occasions.

Once she realised he had ditched her for good he couldn't expect her to keep her mouth shut. Why should she? There were all sorts of unpleasant possibilities. Pretty soon there might be a nation-wide search for a blue Viva. She wouldn't remember the number – there was no reason why she should, just the colour and the make.

On the edge of the New Forest he stopped at a filling station for petrol and cigarettes; there was a café but it wasn't open yet. He trundled along circumspectly, not quite as easy in his mind as before – he couldn't afford to risk keeping the car on the road until he had done something about it. The Viva was a popular model, and plenty of them were blue.

He had the cash to make a quick sale at one of the used-car places, but his name was on the log book, and second-hand dealers were sharp enough to do some quick checking. So that was out.

If he dumped the car somewhere the chances were that it would be found, and attention directed into the area. Not so good either. He had to remain mobile. He was still chewing over the problem when he came to a café that was open for business. He ordered a substantial breakfast, he was the first customer of the day, and while he waited he had time to study an illustrated map of the New Forest area that was displayed on the wall. It was a map aimed at the tourist trade, and it had a heap of useful information – lists of hotels and places of interest, recommended routes … and the location of some caravan camping sites.

It was summer, and most places would be full, hotels wouldn't be likely to have any vacancies, and he needed a place where he wouldn't be noticed, which eliminated the smaller boarding houses. A caravan camp might be just the job. Lots of people and plenty of movement.

So he took some notes of likely places, attacked his breakfast, and then set out on his quest. All the morning he kept at it: Ringwood and Brockenhurst, around and about in all that lovely wooded countryside, every place was full and had been so for weeks; some sites had a No Vacancies sign, but even those he tried and got a quick brush-off. What made it all the more exasperating was that he had the cash to pay well over the odds.

He tried a motel, and the lady at the desk more or less laughed in his face. She said there might be something if he cared to call back later in case there was a cancellation. How late? After ten o'clock that night. It was like getting a room at Buckingham Palace.

He had covered a lot of miles, and the doors had all been shut in his face. The district was too bloody popular, that was the trouble. He had lunch in a pub near Lyndhurst and decided he needed a change of tactics: now if this had been London he would know where to go and who was likely to help. Local information, that was what he was short of.

The waiter who was serving him looked a friendly type, young and quick. Sam had ordered the best the place could provide, with brandy and a cigar to round it off. He paid with a fiver and told the lad to keep the change.

Then he put his problem.

'Leave it to me, sir,' said the waiter. 'I'll see what I can do ... just for yourself?'

'That's it,' said Sam. 'No wife, no kids, just me–'

'Lucky you, sir,' said the waiter. Here was a feller with money to burn and no encumbrances – that wallet of his had been stuffed with cash. The waiter took off. Sam removed himself to the lounge and finished his cigar. There was a daily paper on one of the tables, and he went through it rapidly without finding anything about *'Bernie's Place'*, which helped him to feel like a gentleman of leisure with money in his pocket and not a care in the world. Well almost.

There were a couple of reasonable looking birds in the lounge, and he passed the time speculating about them in an intimate fashion because he was ready to bet they weren't married to the fellers they were with. The blonde with the big knockers wasn't just there for the beer.

The waiter returned, bringing good news. The "Ocean View" caravan camp, near Lymington, had a single-berth caravan.

'You can have it as a special favour, sir,' the waiter whispered. 'I happen to know the manager – you know how it is–'.

'I know,' said Sam, and added another pound note to what he had already donated.

'Thank you, sir. Always a pleasure to be of service. Just tell him I sent you – Ted Williams. Have a nice holiday.'

'You're a good lad,' said Sam genially, and made for the door.

FIVE

'Must be your lucky day,' said the manager at the 'Ocean View'. He was a fat chatty little character, with a little snippet of a beard that didn't go with his plump face and double chin. Harry Harding was the name. A bit of an operator, Sam decided at first sight. 'We're booked solid through the season, couldn't offer you anything in the four-berth or six-berth line … but there is just one single-berth caravan I might be able to arrange, don't get too much call for them, to tell you the absolute truth.'

Harry Harding gave Sam a man-to-man look. 'We run a nice family business here, when we let a single-berth we don't have any hanky-panky, if you see what I mean. It stays a single – you got no idea the way some youngsters act up if they think they can get away with it.'

Sam shook his head at the immorality of modern youth. He had introduced himself as Frank Foster from Cambridge. He had a car, he had luggage, and he had his wallet out and ready.

'I haven't come all this way to chase after birds,' said Sam. 'I just want to relax and take things easy.'

'Very reasonable,' said Harry Harding, and pretended to consult the site diagram on the wall behind his desk.

'There's Number Seventy,' he said. 'A nice little single-berth. As a matter of fact I use it myself sometimes – have to keep an eye on things at night now and then, y'know … it's expected, and I don't like any funny stuff going on. You'll find it's fully equipped, radio, and my own portable telly. Anything you want you can get at our store. How long for, Mr Foster?'

'Maybe a couple of weeks,' said Sam.

Harry Harding frowned. 'That might be a bit inconvenient to arrange,' he said. 'I only do this as a private favour, understand? I wouldn't normally do it for more than the odd night, to oblige … two weeks might be a little difficult, just a little…'

'How much?' said Sam, and he guessed his timing was right. He was as good as home and dried. Harry Harding was on the fiddle, his job was probably supposed to be at least partly resident – and anything he got for the casual renting of Number Seventy would slide right into his own pocket. A fortnight might increase the risk of being found out – Harding would have a boss floating around somewhere. Risks had to be paid for, and Sam understood that as well.

Harry Harding pursed his lips and fingered the end of his little beard. 'We're packed out, you can see that for yourself–'

'You'll be doing me a favour,' said Sam. 'I appreciate it.'

'You'll never get in anywhere else, I know that for a fact,' said Harding. 'How about twenty quid a week?'

'Cash in advance?' Sam smiled and began to count the money out. He didn't expect a receipt and he didn't get one. It was robbery with a smile on both sides.

They drove in Sam's car through the crowded site along a gravelled road in between the lines of family caravans. Number Seventy stood on its own at the end of the main concourse, and it had far more space around it than any of the others. It was clearly a miniature de luxe job.

'You've got your own water and electricity,' Harding pointed out. 'There's no messing about with water buckets or Calor gas. A home from home, as you might say. I tried to get a phone put in but they wouldn't wear it. We run a café if you don't fancy your own cooking.'

He unlocked the caravan and showed Sam all the amenities. Between them they occupied most of the limited space, but all the essentials were there, and Sam was happy to note that he wouldn't be hemmed in by neighbours too closely. Just a few yards away there was the fence that surrounded the site, and a wood beyond.

'You can be as private here as you like,' said Harding. 'Nobody to bother you.'

'Suits me,' said Sam, and wished the gabby bastard would leave.

'We don't have a liquor licence,' said Harding, 'but I keep a little supply, so if you ever run short, you know where to come.'

Sam told him he would keep it in mind, and finally got rid of him by saying he wanted to clean himself up after that long drive down from Cambridge. He did in fact heat some water and give himself a quick shave. That suitcase with the money was going to be a real problem.

That shifty git of a manager certainly had a key to the caravan, and any time he saw Sam drive out he was more than likely to let himself in and sniff around. The lock on the case was nothing much, and if Harry-Bleeding-Harding came across all that cash under Sam's shirts he would start getting ideas that Sam wouldn't welcome: he had been right about Harry Harding – he was an operator and a crude one at that, so he would have to be watched, and not given any cause to stick his nose in where Sam wouldn't want it.

He made a cursory examination of the caravan; there was no place there where he might hide a biggish bundle of notes, not without shifting some of the wall panels, and that was just the kind of thing Harding would notice first go off.

The boot of the car would be safer, as long as he made sure to leave the car where he could keep an eye on it, and that might not always be possible. It was a problem. An embarrassment of riches, unusual for Sam Harris.

He strolled through the site to the store and collected a small stock of groceries. He noted that he was the only man in the place in a suit, he would have to do something about that if he didn't want to stick out too obviously as a newcomer. He had to blend with the general surroundings. A bloke on holiday. Just like anybody else. No birds? Well, that remained to be seen. He had the money to spend, and birds meant money.

He found some old newspapers in one of the drawers, and wrapped the money into a neat packet. He put it in the boot of the car, under the tool kit. On his way out of the site he waved at Harry Harding who was standing in the doorway of his office just by the main entrance. He had left his suitcase in the caravan on the small folding table, and he would know if it had been messed about when he got back. Harding was welcome to try his luck. There was nothing in the case that would identify him as Sam Harris.

He found Lymington crowded, cars on each side of the main street, right the way down the slope leading to the water. It was a sunny afternoon, and he had to nose into a side street before he could find an empty slot for the car. He liked the look of the place – pavements full of people drifting about in holiday gear.

In a gents outfitters in the main street he bought some bright shirts and two pairs of striped slacks and a beige summer-weight coat. He sat over a cup of coffee in the upstairs room of a café where he had a good view of the street below. There was money about. Outside the pub opposite there was a maroon Rolls, a couple of elderly characters came out of the pub and climbed into the Rolls, followed by a long-legged lovely in brief white shorts and a spotted blue jersey – loose blonde hair and nicely tanned, just the way Sam fancied them. He watched her chatting to the duchess in the front seat – her mum? Dad said something that made them all laugh, the bird went off down the slope and the Rolls pulled majestically out into the traffic.

The pub might be a good place for food, and Sam didn't intend to do much cooking for himself. Before he drove back he bought some sun-glasses. A couple of weeks in the sunshine, keeping his nose clean and bothering nobody – there couldn't be anything wrong with that. It would give him time to work out what he was going to do next.

Round about now Lily would start wondering where he was. She would be expecting him back with Percy – or did she know better than that already? Had Freddie Stainer given the fuzz his name? Was Sam Harris being spread about?

He went into a paper shop, they had no London dailies left and they didn't get the evening editions. He drove back. His case hadn't been disturbed. He had missed the five o'clock news on the radio, the portable telly was on the blink, no matter how much he fiddled with it. He passed the time by changing into some of his new gear.

His nearest neighbours had returned from wherever they had been spending the day. There were three noisy kids and a dog with a loud bark and superfluous energy; they had a coloured ball and the kids were kicking it about and that goddamn yapping dog was chasing after it all over the place. Peace and relaxation! Not a hope.

Sam opened his door to invite them to belt up, but he got sight of their dad – six foot four with arms down to his knees. He withdrew and shut all his windows and the caravan began to heat up. He'd have to lay in a stock of light ale, and he wouldn't get it from Harry Harding either – he had made his contribution to that small-time racketeer. Enough was enough.

The six o'clock news came up. International and domestic crises, all the usual stuff. Right at the tail end was the bit Sam had been waiting for.

Following an anonymous phone tip-off in the early hours of the morning, the police had called at a well-known social club in the home counties, *'Bernie's Place'*. In the car park they had found the body of a man, later identified as Frederick Stainer, an employee at the club; the nature of his injuries suggested that he had been run over by a vehicle; he had died in the ambulance on the way to the hospital.

In the car park the police had come across a bag with an unspecified sum of money.

In the manager's office there had been the dead body of a man, so far unidentified; he had been shot and a gun had been found in the room.

The door of the strong-room and the safe in the office had been expertly burgled, and the contents rifled. The thieves had decamped, leaving the apparatus behind – possibly after being disturbed.

According to a police spokesman, at least one other member of a gang must have been involved, and the police were anxious to interview anyone who had been in the vicinity of the club and so on and so forth...

It was a bit of a shaker – that soft bump when he was getting under way must have been Freddie Stainer under the back wheel. Sam ran some water into the small basin and cooled his face. And he didn't feel very good.

It had been an accident. It hadn't been his fault. Stainer had been crazy mad, hanging on to the door of the car like that ... all he'd tried to do was shake him off, not kill him! Anybody who'd been there could see that it hadn't been Sam's fault ... but there hadn't been anybody else, only Sam and nobody was going to take his word for it, he knew that only too well.

If they got him he'd be right in the dirt. Had Stainer talked to the police before he kicked it? They'd have had a copper riding in the ambulance. Always did in messes like this.

And another thing – they would identify Percy pretty soon, they had his prints on record, so if they started shoving the name of Percy Cater around Lily might hear it – she didn't bother much with newspapers, but she always had the radio on.

She'd be a bit stirred up because they hadn't come back, and he wished he'd given her a better story – he should have said they'd be away for a week or so. He had taken most of his clothes, so she knew he wasn't coming back.

She was no kid, would she chalk it up to experience? You never could tell with women. All he could do was hope she didn't hear the name of Percy Cater on the radio.

He couldn't spend the rest of a fine evening sweltering in his little caravan, brooding over what he couldn't help and chewing his fingers. He needed company. Good grub and couple of snorts. He'd never sleep otherwise.

Just a little reasonable luck, that was all he asked for. Percy was dead and Stainer was dead and none of it had been really Sam's fault, and most of the cash hadn't been nicked after all, so Sam thought it would be only right if a little luck came his way.

The fact that he and Percy had intended to diddle Stainer out of his slice didn't weigh much on Sam's elastic conscience. He drove back into the town. It was too early to eat, and if he sat in a bar he was feeling so low that he just might get stoned, and that might not be a good idea.

He found a space for the car, and walked down to look at the water. There were boats of all sizes bobbing and jinking at their moorings. Sam was no sailor: standing on the end of a pier in a stiff breeze could make him queasy. But he had to admit that the boats made a pretty sight, and they weren't all of them little sailing jobs either. There were cabin cruisers, with sun decks and cocktail lounges; you'd need a crew to run them and a very deep pocket – but you could nip across to France or Spain, or fetch up in the fun spots along the Mediterranean. Some people knew how to live all right.

He watched a party being rowed to the landing stage from one of the big cruisers moored some way out. There were two men and a couple of girls, which looked like a sensible arrangement to Sam. There were plenty of birds dotted around, and some of them were easy to watch in their jeans. It must be something about the sea air that gave them an extra saucy appearance.

As the dinghy drew nearer to the landing stage Sam found his interest fixed on one of the men, the one who wasn't doing the rowing.

A few years back, and a for a brief and eventually unprofitable period, Sam had tried to slide his way into the operations of a certain Phil Harrigan who was then tipped as a character with a big future. It had not worked out well for Sam, because even then Harrigan had been right out of Sam's modest league and soon made it clear he positively had no use for Sam's services.

The current whisper now was that Phil Harrigan had become Mister Big, the brain behind most of the enterprises that made headlines and showed a large profit. The man with a finger in many pies, he had the skill and the resources to keep himself in the clear. He operated by remote control, and as far as Sam had ever heard, he had never been pulled in for questioning.

He was in the position where he could buy information, and it was commonly believed – not without reason – that some ranking members of the fuzz were on his unofficial payroll.

Sam himself had never got beyond the outer fringes of the Harrigan organization. He had quite simply failed to measure up to Harrigan's very special requirements. He had none of the skills or the toughness Harrigan demanded in his underlings, and he had afterwards thought himself lucky to get away without having any of his moving parts damaged beyond repair. And he had never had the nerve to try again. He wasn't that crazy.

Harrigan paid well, true enough, but he ran a disciplined outfit, and there were some nasty stories about what happened when somebody didn't deliver – or tried to develop private ambitions. It didn't stop at a broken leg or a routine beating up by the muscle men: the unfortunate offender just wasn't around any more.

With mounting interest Sam watched the big feller down there helping the girls up out of the little boat. He was the spitting image of Phil Harrigan. Hefty and tough and handsome in a brutal sort of way. The black beard was new, but he stood and moved around just the way Harrigan did – like a boss, the bloke who said jump and everybody jumped. Or else.

He had slung his arm around one of the girls and she wasn't objecting. She was a blonde in tight jeans and bulky sweater, the kind of bird Sam would have chosen himself. She was laughing as they made their way along the swaying wooden planks, and Sam reckoned he knew what they'd probably been doing out there on that nice big boat.

He was remembering that Phil Harrigan was a great boy for a party when he was in the mood. Sam had never been to one because he hadn't made the grade in the outfit, but he knew the form: lashings of booze and amenable birds.

The other man had tied up the dingy, he was carrying a zip bag, and he trailed along after the other three. Sam was sure he hadn't seen him before. But then Harrigan had a long payroll. And maybe this wasn't Harrigan, just a bloke with a beard who looked like him.

Sam had never heard that Harrigan went in for this sea-faring stuff. If he could get close enough to hear his voice he'd know if it was Phil Harrigan.

He didn't intend to introduce himself. If that really was Harrigan, he had one of those fabulous memories, he would remember Sam, and it wouldn't be with any favour. Also Sam fancied he had enough on his mind to be going on with.

He watched the four of them cross the grass to where the cars were parked, but when he saw they were walking on up into the town he followed – just to find out if it was Phil Harrigan. The yachting scene didn't quite fit the Harrigan image.

It was easy to keep them in sight at a discreet distance. Sam had done this kind of thing many times before, and he had plenty of strollers on the pavement to give him cover. But none of them turned round, and Sam had ample time to appreciate the neat rear view of the blonde with the bloke who just might be Phil Harrigan. The other one was no eyesore either, a bit plumpish – she wasn't doing as much laughing as the blonde.

All four of them turned into the pub Sam had noted as a possible place to feed. He drifted past and looked in the windows of the neighbouring shops.

He smoked a cigarette. Common sense told him to leave it strictly alone. Phil Harrigan was bad news if you didn't happen to be part of the outfit. The thought that it might be Harrigan niggled at Sam. No harm in finding out. He wouldn't take any risks. They wouldn't even know.

He wandered into the entrance. The dining-room was on the left and he could see through the glass door. Some of the tables were occupied, but not by the party he was after.

This wasn't just a pub, it had residential accommodation upstairs, and there was a notice at the bottom of the stairs: *Residents Lounge.* The hotel office was in front of him, and there was a girl working over her accounts – and another sign: *No vacancies.*

On the right was the lounge bar, doing a nice business with mostly sailing types – but he couldn't see his four. It looked like the kind of place where the beer might be drinkable, judging by the tankards some of those hearty characters were handling. Sam got himself a pint, for starters, and settled at a table by the window. There were worse ways of passing time.

Pity he couldn't get himself a room in the place, it would be an improvement on the rabbit hutch he had rented. He was attending to his beer when he saw the girl coming across from the stairs. Not the blonde, the other one. She had changed into a dress, and she didn't seem so plump, just nicely covered and healthy. Darkish hair and pretty nice legs under a very short skirt. She wasn't alone. The man who had carried the luggage was with her. He had put on a dark blue blazer and dark slacks; square-shouldered and with a dark chin and thick eyebrows, he didn't look a sociable type.

He didn't ask the girl what she was drinking, just made for the bar, and Sam thought he would be one of those awkward characters who always got to the front of a busy bar, and got quick attention.

He was and he did. The girl had taken a seat at an empty table next to the one Sam was at. Sam picked up a copy of the Yachting World and became absorbed in it. A gin and tonic arrived for the girl, and she nodded her thanks. Her companion took a seat with his back to Sam. He was drinking whisky.

The girl tried her drink. 'They forgot the gin,' she said.

'Don't bitch. I've had enough for one day.'

'You think I've enjoyed it?' The girl's voice was sharp.

'Part of the job.' The man shrugged. 'The

rough with the smooth. You're being childish, Anne. Even he noticed. He told me not to bring you next time.'

Anne had lit a cigarette. 'Dear God,' she said savagely. 'Phil says the word so you roll over and play dead! You sicken me!'

'Shut up,' he said. 'You get on my nerves.'

'And just what do you think you do to me, Jerry?' she demanded. 'Just because I'm your wife it doesn't mean I have to pretend I enjoy a trip like the one we've just been through – there are limits.'

She laughed harshly, and went on in a fierce whisper, 'Your boss and his girl-friend! I found it quite revolting.'

Eavesdropping was one of Sam's private talents, frequently exercised, but seldom to better advantage than now. Anne and Jerry. Husband and wife, having a good old marital bull-and-cow. Phil was in it somewhere. Phil Harrigan? Of course, Sam was sure of that now.

They had momentarily lowered their voices. There was a hostile pause in the argument. Sam kept his eyes on the yachting magazine, his ears flapping.

'Another drink?' said Jerry.

'Are we allowed to eat?' she said frostily.

'I've booked.'

'Just the two of us, I hope? I couldn't stand another dose of Phil and his Diana.'

'You're prejudiced,' said her husband.

93

'It's an insult to me,' she said, 'including me in a party with that whore–'

Jerry laughed very softly, and Sam could see his shoulders shaking. He also noted the fresh sparkle in Anne's eyes. Few women can stand being laughed at, even Sam knew that much. For a moment he thought she was about to chuck the remains of her drink into her husband's face. No such luck.

'Everybody's in it for the money,' said Jerry. 'Diana's all right, at least she's honest about it–'

'She's a bore,' said Anne.

'Phil doesn't think so.'

'A month from now he won't remember what she looked like.'

'He would just love to know that his private affairs interested you so much,' said Jerry.

'Since you're his lackey,' she said sweetly, 'that isn't surprising ... don't tell me you fancy her yourself?'

Her husband leaned back in his chair, making it creak. There was plenty of muscle there.

'Bitch,' he said softly.

'That's better,' she murmured. Sam glanced across just in time to see the sudden smile that softened her face. She reached across the table and touched his hand. A gesture of reconciliation just when Sam had been expecting fireworks? You never could tell with some married couples.

Sam missed the next piece of dialogue because some comic clot at the bar had just told a dirty one and the chesty guffaws drowned out everything else.

'...I have to go out afterwards,' Jerry was saying impatiently. 'You know that. You know why we're here ... so for heaven's sake give it a rest–'

'You're doing his dirty work again,' she said. 'Let me come with you.'

'You're being childish,' he said. 'Finish your drink and let's eat.'

'I wish you had more guts,' she said.

'I don't see you refusing the money.' He stood up, and then for the first time he looked around, and Sam buried himself in his magazine and hoped he didn't look like a bloke who would listen into a private conversation between husband and wife.

He watched them cross to the dining-room, and from the way Jerry was moving he looked as ready to strangle his missus as feed her. Sam thought it had all the marks of an interesting situation: Jerry had to do some dirty work and Anne didn't approve. And Phil Harrigan was pulling the strings? That was more than likely.

Sam reflected on the possibilities. He had to eat somewhere. And he assumed that Phil Harrigan and his bird wouldn't be joining those two. He let a few minutes pass, and strolled into the dining-room. It had filled up. He hadn't booked, he was a non-resident, so the waitress put him at a less-favoured table in a corner.

He could watch Jerry and Anne, after a fashion, but he hadn't a hope of hearing anything. They were still arguing, and she was doing most of it.

SIX

The service was slow. There weren't enough waitresses and they looked like students doing vacation jobs. Sam was in no hurry, and the girl who was looking after him was friendly even if a little slap-dash.

Eileen was the name, as Sam soon discovered. A big girl with a ready smile – the kind of girl who just might be willing to gossip a little about the hotel and its clients.

Sam was half-way through his meal when he looked up and suddenly lost his appetite as he saw Phil Harrigan stalk in, looking very modish in a dark suit of a beautiful cut. He swept past Sam's table, halted and nodded at Anne, and bent over Jerry. He said something very briefly, patted Jerry on the shoulder, and went out.

Through the glass door Sam caught a

fleeting glimpse of the lush blonde, Diana, with some kind of a fur wrap trailing over one bare shoulder and looking very exclusive, as she waited for Harrigan, and a few moments afterwards there was the sound of a nice engine accelerating up the street. Phil Harrigan always allowed himself the best in transport, varying his vehicle to suit the occasion – this might be the night for the latest mark of Jag. Diana, stripped to the essentials for a social evening, was probably a Jag bird.

The bitter conflict between Jerry and Anne had been renewed. She was pleading with him, and not getting any joy, leaning forward across the table, until she finally became aware that the diners at the next table had suspended their operations to listen – and Sam was wishing he was among them.

Anne, her face flushed and her eyes stormy, got up and marched out of the room. Jerry lit a cigarette and stared at the littered table. When he glanced at the interested spectators at the next table his expression was so hostile that Sam hoped he would clout somebody.

He mightn't be one of Harrigan's muscle boys, but he clearly wasn't the sort of feller any sensible citizen would want to mess about with.

Sam was disappointed. Nobody got clobbered. Jerry glared his fill and wasn't challenged. He left. Eileen had reached Sam's table with his coffee.

'You see that?' said Sam. 'Some drama – are they staying here?'

Eileen nodded. 'Mr and Mrs Winters ... something upset her, she's rather sweet, I've never known them quarrel like that...'

'That feller who came in just now,' said Sam, 'with the beard, that was Phil Harrigan, wasn't it?'

'Oh him!' said Eileen and began to collect the dishes. 'Plenty of money – I'll say no more if he's a friend of yours–'

'He can break a leg for all I care,' said Sam.

Eileen giggled and stacked her tray.

'Is he staying here as well?' said Sam, 'and the blonde?'

'Off and on,' said Eileen. 'Excuse me.' She went off with her load. Sam smoked a cigarette and waited for her to bring his bill. Eileen was worth cultivating, just for the hell of it.

So Phil Harrigan had not endeared himself to the domestic staff. Sam wasn't surprised. Harrigan pushed people around, he thought money paid for everything, especially the hired help who couldn't afford to tell him to jump in the lake. To Harrigan ordinary folk were so much trash, which made him an easy man not to like.

Sam had been keeping a sharp eye on the glass door of the dining-room, and he knew that neither Anne Winters nor her husband had left the hotel, at least by the front door. He surmised they were probably continuing their fight in the privacy of their room, and his money was on the lady – the waitress approved of her, which was a point in her favour.

Eileen arrived with his bill. Sam added a pound to the total. Eileen didn't refuse the tip, but she gave Sam a very straight look, and said very softly, 'we're not supposed to gossip about the guests – I'm only temporary here, but I don't want to lose the job...'

'Understood,' said Sam just as quietly. 'You won't get into any trouble over me, I promise you – I just happen to be sort of interested in Phil Harrigan, and anybody who knocks about in his company... I'm not a policeman or anything like that–'

Eileen allowed another little giggle to escape. 'I didn't think you were ... you don't look like one...'

Sam was grinning as he rose from the table. 'You couldn't have said a nicer thing – I'd never fool a smart girl like you–'

'I don't miss much,' she murmured.

'Might look in tomorrow some time – so anything you happen to hear – okay?'

She nodded, and Sam left and he was thinking that he had recruited a useful source of information. It was a small place, and the staff would know what was going on. So he could keep tabs on Phil Harrigan without sticking his neck out.

He was standing on the pavement outside the hotel, reflecting that it was still a bit early to lock himself up in his caravan on a fine summer night. This wasn't, he concluded morosely, the kind of place where he'd pick up the right sort of female to comfort his lonely state. It would need some research, maybe tomorrow when he'd had the time to inspect the territory. If there was any spare talent about Sam would find it.

He was distracted by the sight of Jerry Winters coming out of the hotel, alone. He had a small case, and without looking to right or left he set off briskly along the pavement, and Sam was remembering that Mrs Winters hadn't been exactly enthusiastic about her husband going out. She had wanted to go with him. And then there had been that bit about Harrigan's dirty work.

Sam didn't need any time to make up his mind. He followed. His car was parked down there anyway. He saw Jerry Winters unlocking a small sports job that was only a few cars down from his own. Sam couldn't resist it.

When Winters pulled away from the kerb Sam did the same, and they drove through the town. Once they got clear of the main traffic Sam expected to be left behind, because Jerry Winters was driving a Sprite, and Sam couldn't hope to keep in touch with his Viva.

A young feller in a bad temper after a quarrel with his wife would sure belt along, and in a sports job as well. But Jerry Winters showed no sign of being in a hurry. He kept to an even speed, as though following a time-table. It made him easy to follow, and Sam was pretty confident he hadn't been noticed. There was no need to follow too closely, and they were not alone on the road.

Through Lyndhurst, and on to Ringwood, and nowhere even on the straight stretches did the Sprite do anything that Sam's Viva couldn't cope with. Some miles the other side of Ringwood they began to leave the main roads, and now Sam had to sit up and pay attention, because of the country cross-roads and sudden junctions that whipped up in front of them, and the warnings about the straying ponies here and there on the grass verges.

He had guessed they might be heading for Salisbury, but not now – and nowhere did Jerry Winters hesitate, right into the heart of the Forest.

Sam was now feeling just a shade anxious. It would be too easy to lose the Sprite here, and if he got too close Winters was likely to wonder why he didn't pass after all those miles up and down.

Down in a dip with the trees all around, Sam lost sight of the Sprite's lights, but as he began to speed up he saw the lane on the left and the outline of the car, now without any lights. He drove on, the road levelled, and there was a grass space. He stopped, and turned off his lights and listened.

If Winters had spotted him, he'd wait a while in that lane. Sam locked the Viva; there was no sound, just odd country night noises in the trees. The Sprite didn't come roaring by.

The clear starlit sky wasn't much comfort, a nice thick fog would have suited him better. He'd come a hell of a long way, tailing after Jerry Winters – there had to be some point to it.

Walking very carefully, he went back, and the minute he heard that Sprite start up he'd beat even time to the nearest bush, and the road was lined with them. When he reached the lane the Sprite was still there and he knew it was empty. All the same, he approached it with much caution. And just to be on the safe side, he let some of the poundage out of the nearside front tyre – if it came to a chase Sam thought his Viva might need some help.

The lane wound out of sight. There were high banks. He climbed up and saw the dark huddle of buildings some hundred yards distant, farm buildings, and beyond them a house of some size with lights – no run of the mill farm either, not with a house that size. He saw some tidy white fencing, and a dark piece of level ground that had to be a nice lawn. The long low buildings would be barns, or stables, or cowsheds.

If Jerry Winters was visiting there he hadn't come by invitation, leaving his car there in the lane. Sam found some shelter behind a wall, and he had barely picked on the right spot to see what it was all in aid of when he noticed out there a stooping figure running like mad in his general direction and he soon knew it was Jerry Winters, and he was coming across that bit of ground a hell of a sight faster than Sam could hope to manage.

So Sam squeezed himself down behind that wall and waited for Winters to pounce on him and rough him up. He heard him panting like a steam engine, and the thudding of his feet over the thick grass.

Winters vaulted the wall a few yards from where Sam squatted. He landed neatly and without looking round went off for the hedge at a fast gallop. Sam popped his head up to see who was chasing after Jerry Winters, and there was nobody.

Then from the direction of the farm buildings he heard some kind of a soft explosion – a *whooshing* noise like a rocket about to take off. And seconds later there were flames leaping about inside there and lighting it all up. It was so unexpected and weird that Sam just stood there by the wall and gaped at the spectacle – and he wouldn't have believed that a place could go up in flames so quickly. It wasn't until he heard the noises of animals in a panic – horses and cows kicking up one hell of a row – that Sam decided to do what he always did in a perilous situation: he prepared to remove himself forthwith. Some men had now reached the burning buildings and they were rushing about, they'd know what to do about rescuing the animals.

He was some yards short of the hedge when he heard the Sprite start, and its gearbox whined as Winters reversed. When its lights came on Sam saw that Winters wasn't going back the way they had come, so he would pass the Viva parked on the grass. Sam wished him the best of luck with one soft front tyre.

This was obviously the 'dirty work' Anne Winters had been beefing about, and her husband had done it. Sam had been engaged in a variety of unlawful enterprises in his time, but arson had never been one of them.

He slithered down the bank and accelerated down the lane. This was going to be no place for any wandering stranger who couldn't explain his presence, not without mentioning the activities of Jerry Winters, and Sam didn't think that might be healthy.

He found the Viva all right, clambered in and surged off along the road. This was no time to dawdle. Direction didn't matter, just speed. Round the second of a series of sharp bends he braked suddenly, because the Sprite lay on its side in the ditch. Jerry Winters, dazed and with blood on his face, was leaning against the wreck. He staggered over, his eyes screwed up, and he had to hold on to the Viva.

'Could you give me a lift?' he said thickly. 'Had a bit of a spill ... tyre must have burst...'

'Hop in,' said Sam. 'How do you feel?'

'Not too good.' Jerry Winters got himself painfully in beside Sam. 'She wouldn't take the corner and I banged my head... I'll be all right in a minute.' He took out a hand-kerchief and dabbed at the cut on his fore-head.

Sam got under way again. This would take some handling. 'Like me to take you to a doctor?' he asked.

'No, that won't be necessary, thanks very much ... lucky for me you came along.'

Sam put on more speed. 'Bit of fuss back there, looked like a fire.'

Jerry Winters said nothing, holding the wadded handkerchief to his face, and Sam thought he had his eyes closed – it couldn't have been much fun when that flabby tyre tipped the car into the ditch. He might have a bit of concussion. He certainly sat there very still and unresponsive as though he didn't give a cuss what happened.

Sam was looking for a sign-post back to civilisation. Pretty soon there would be plenty of official traffic in the area – fire appliances and squad cars, and he had the cause of it all sitting there beside him. Some fun.

He put a dozen fast miles behind them. They whipped through some sleeping hamlets, and Sam drove as though he knew just where they were going, which was not quite the case.

Winters roused himself and mumbled something about wanting to be sick, so Sam stopped and let him get out, and he got rid of most of the dinner Sam had seen him eat. He was appreciably better afterwards.

'Where are we going?' he asked.

'Where would you like?' said Sam. 'The fire's a long way behind us now – wasn't that what you wanted?'

'Why do you say that?' There was nothing rambling about Jerry Winters' voice now.

'Come off it,' said Sam. 'You started the fire.'

Winters peered at him. 'I've seen you before,' he said slowly.

'In the pub, tonight, your wife's name is Anne – you should have listened to her, Jerry:

that was a dirty job you did back there, and I know who sent you.'

Sam didn't need to glance at Winters to know he was ringing the bell loud and clear.

'Just who are you?' said Winters.

'Doest it matter?' said Sam. 'You're the boy we have to worry about right now ... you feel happy about what you just did?'

'My God,' said Winters. 'You mean he sent you after me to check on me? I never thought he'd do that!'

Sam had slowed a little, because this might become awkward, and he was remembering the way Jerry had glared at those innocent customers who had shown an interest in his row with his wife at dinner, and Sam didn't want to get himself clobbered.

Winters fumbled for his cigarette case, his eyes fixed on Sam who was happy to note how his hand shook when he gave himself a light. Jerry was suddenly a very worried young man, and not so tough after all.

If he thought Sam was part of Phil Harrigan's shadow mob, that meant he was new to the game.

'Your first time out on your own?' said Sam.

'I don't know what you're getting at.' Jerry Winters pulled nervously at his cigarette.

'The man won't like it if the fuzz take you in,' said Sam. 'You won't get your bonus–'

'It was that blasted car!' Winters interrupted explosively. 'It was all right until I went off the road – I'd have been clean away if that hadn't happened!'

'And you left the car behind,' Sam reminded him.

'Hell, what else could I do?'

'I know what I'd do,' said Sam. 'I'd call on the police in the morning and report that my car was stolen in the night – they might believe you if you don't happen to have any record with them, because sure as hell they'll check any vehicle found in that area back there, so if you have any form with the police you're really in the dirt.'

'I have no police record,' said Winters stiffly.

'I hope you can keep it that way,' said Sam politely. 'So report a stolen car and keep your fingers crossed. Your wife will back you up, won't she? Wives usually do – although that was a pretty lousy job you did – you didn't wait to hear those animals screaming, it won't make very nice reading in the paper … people don't go much on cruelty to animals–'

'The place was supposed to be empty,' said Winters.

'And now you know damn well it wasn't,' said Sam. 'Doesn't that bother you at all?'

'Just shut up and drive!' said Winters.

'You don't scare me, boy.' It was not quite true, but Sam was hoping he had made it sound right. He thought he had Winters nervous and off balance, so a frontal attack might be the answer. 'You can get out and start walking home any time you like. I won't lose any sleep over it – I don't much fancy the kind of bloke who uses an incendiary bomb on animals... I'm not fussy, but I reckon I'd draw the line at that–'

'For a little squirt you talk pretty big,' said Winters. 'The barns were supposed to be empty. I wouldn't have done it otherwise... I don't know why the hell I'm explaining myself to you, I don't know who you are or what your status is.'

'How long have you been working for Phil Harrigan?'

Sam slipped the question in. Until then neither of them had mentioned the name. Jerry Winters glanced at Sam, tossed his cigarette out of the window, and made no reply. Now he really was puzzled.

'I bet Phil has covered himself for tonight, with Diana,' said Sam. 'I bet he's got a flock of witnesses ready to swear he was nowhere near the spot where you set that bomb off. Good old Phil, everybody else may get left in the dirt, not Phil.'

'You seem to know a lot about him,' said Winters. His tone was guarded. 'But you still haven't explained yourself.'

'You could say I'm your good luck for the night,' said Sam.

'I've never heard him mention anybody who fits your description,' said Winters. 'He didn't send you after me, did he?'

'That's for you to worry over,' said Sam. 'Where did Phil take Diana? London?'

'Near enough,' said Winters. 'Some private club where he can gamble, he won't be coming back for a couple of days–'

'And in the meantime you and your wife have a little respectable holiday by the sea. Does she know what kind of a lousy crook you are? You needn't answer that. But just tell me this – what was that fire in aid of? Who owns the place? You might as well tell me, because I'll hear all about it on the telly and read about it in the papers. Arson's a fairly dirty line of business. Phil Harrigan put you on to it, so tell me why.'

'Suppose I tell you to mind your own business?' said Winters, his self-confidence coming back to him. 'From the act you put on I thought you were the man with all the answers, but now I don't think you can be anybody I have to give answers to … so you can get knotted.'

'Well now,' said Sam, 'I might be a law-abiding citizen, I might be anxious to see a dirty crook handed over to justice.'

'You're quite the little comedian,' said Winters.

'This is the position,' said Sam. 'I can deliver you nice and snug back to your hotel inside an hour or so, or I can stop at the next police station and say my piece – pick your choice, boyo.'

'I don't understand your interest,' said Winters. 'You don't work for Phil Harrigan – and you seem to know things you don't need to know.'

'The story of my life,' said Sam. 'Incidentally, if you're thinking of sticking one on me, I don't advise it, because it wouldn't do you any good unless you made it permanent – and that wouldn't be quite your scene, would it?'

'Don't push me too far,' said Winters. 'I could make you unhappy for long enough.'

'I don't doubt it,' said Sam. 'You're younger and you're bigger – but you couldn't stop me remembering what happened tonight, you get the picture?'

'I'll have to talk to Phil first,' said Winters. 'He doesn't like his business being spread around, least of all to a man who doesn't have a name–'

'But who came along just in time,' said Sam.

'Having followed me all the way,' said Winters.

'Don't forget to tell Phil you didn't know I was right there on your tail, he'll nail you to the fence.'

Jerry Winters slumped down in his seat, a very morose young man.

'One thing I will say for old Phil,' Sam went on cheerfully, 'he pays for service, and he expects service, so after tonight I wouldn't reckon your standing will be too high – I didn't know Phil went in for arson, it's a bit crude for him … and he puts a mug like you on the job.'

'We had the wrong information, that's all,' said Winters wearily.

'Phil never gets the wrong information,' said Sam. 'He stays out of trouble that way – and makes plenty of money. You started a fire in a building with animals inside there, horses and cows and Lord knows what else, and you tell me you thought it was empty. You must be a proper Charlie.'

'I was just carrying out orders,' said Winters listlessly. 'I'm sick of the whole damned business.'

'I bet those animals didn't enjoy it much either,' said Sam. 'Where was the profit for Phil? What did he get out of it?'

Winters shot him a guarded look. 'You're asking a lot of questions, whoever you are.'

'Put yourself in my place,' said Sam. 'Wouldn't you want to know what the hell was going on?'

'You're some kind of a crook yourself,' said Winters. 'That's obvious.'

'I wouldn't set fire to a bunch of helpless animals,' said Sam. 'So don't let's chuck so much dirt around. If anybody told me to set

112

fire to a farm building in the middle of the night I'd make bloody sure there was nothing inside it.'

'I was in a hurry,' said Winters.

'You were scared,' said Sam. 'You're still scared, boyo. You're in the wrong line of business.'

Jerry Winters laughed, a harsh joyless sound. 'You could be right. I've never done anything like this before – and I won't again.'

'I wouldn't bet on it,' said Sam. 'Not if you stick with Phil Harrigan … you know the roads around here?'

'Are you taking me back to Lymington?'

'Why not?' said Sam. 'I'm lumbered with you.'

'I'm grateful,' said Winters.

'You should be,' said Sam.

SEVEN

They came to a left turn, and under Winters' directions they avoided Blandford and were on the Ringwood road after some twisting miles that kept Sam busy. It would be after midnight when they reached Lymington, but Winters said they knew at the hotel that he would be out late.

'When do you report to Harrigan?' said Sam.

'I don't,' said Winters. 'We're supposed to be on holiday, I've got the use of his cruiser and he's paying the hotel bills and so on.'

'He's got you on a string,' said Sam. 'You should listen to your wife more often, she's got sense.'

'I don't know why she sticks with me,' said Winters. 'I'm no good to her, God knows I'm not—'

'You'll have me crying in a minute,' said Sam. 'For a feller who chucks fire-bombs around you're pretty sorry for yourself all of a sudden, I don't get it.'

'It was just part of a campaign,' said Winters. 'Phil thought it up – it was meant to be a sharp reminder to somebody who's been lining himself up against Harrigan and trying to make things difficult ... isn't that enough for you? You must know what happens when Phil meets with any opposition.'

'I know,' said Sam.

'It began as a business feud,' said Winters. 'Phil doesn't like anybody getting in his hair, something had to be done, there was nobody else available, so I got the job, and I wish now I'd had the guts to say no!'

'Phil doesn't like people who turn him down,' said Sam. 'I hear they don't live very long afterwards, maybe that's just a rumour. What does he normally pay you for? You're no muscle boy, they come ten a penny – you might be a con merchant, but I doubt that, you don't have the nerve … so what do you do?'

'I help to keep some of his books straight,' said Winters. 'Straight enough to fool the Inland Revenue, and if you think that's easy you don't know what I'm talking about. I'm a chartered accountant – or I was. I'm no fire-raiser.'

'So get another job,' said Sam. 'I thought accountants were like lawyers, always in the money.'

'I had a little trouble in South Africa,' said Winters. 'Money trouble.'

'You got theirs mixed up with yours?' said Sam. 'I hear it happens.'

'They call it misappropriation,' said Winters wryly. 'Fraudulent conversion. I couldn't put it back in time and I got caught.'

'Sloppy,' said Sam. 'And you a bloke with brains.'

'I miscalculated, I was too optimistic,' said Winters.

'The jails are full of blokes like you,' said Sam. 'So look where you ended up, working for a crook like Phil Harrigan.'

'I told you I haven't any record with the police over here, and it's true,' said Winters. 'But when I served my time they shipped me out, and I haven't been able to land another decent job. They all want references,

115

and I can't supply them – a three-year spell in a South African prison doesn't make the right impression on a prospective employer, especially when the job involves handling large sums of money, his money.

'I was in pretty low water when I met up with Phil Harrigan and he offered me a job.'

'Cooking the books,' said Sam.

'It wasn't quite like that at first,' said Winters. 'You know him, so you'll know how pleasant and convincing he can be when he feels like it.'

'I also know what a king-bastard he is,' said Sam with relish.

'I found that out for myself later on. Anne and I got married on the strength of the money he was paying me. I would never have got it from any respectable firm.'

'Didn't that tell you anything? Phil doesn't run an organization to put cons on their feet. He's a high-powered operator.'

'I discovered that as well,' said Winters. 'But by then I was involved up to my neck, and I owe him money, for the flat we live in and most of the furniture.'

'He's got his hooks in you all right,' said Sam. 'You must be good at fiddling the books or he wouldn't have put out any cash, not Phil Harrigan.'

'Any trained accountant can do it,' said Winters. 'You just have to be basically dishonest, and I suppose I must be a natural-born crook.'

Sam laughed. 'Don't kid yourself. You'd never make the grade with real operators in a hundred years. You're jail-bait all right, I grant you that–'

'Thanks.'

'You're welcome,' said Sam. 'Look at tonight: if somebody else had come along and picked you out of the ditch, with that farm going up in flames a couple of hundred yards away, you'd probably be spending the night in a cell somewhere while they sorted you out.'

'Do you think I don't know that?' said Winters.

'Your wife wants you to pack it in, doesn't she?' said Sam. 'How much does she know?'

'Enough to have her worried sick,' said Winters. 'She never liked Harrigan.'

'She's smarter than you. Phil reckons he's sudden death to a bird with any looks, and your wife is no old bag–'

'Thanks again. Could we talk of something else? I don't think I care to discuss my wife in these circumstances – it was her bad luck to marry me, let's leave it at that.'

'She'll walk out on you one of these days,' said Sam.

'If you must talk,' said Winters abruptly, 'find another topic.'

'Like who owns the place you set on fire?' said Sam. 'This feller who's been getting in

Phil's way? Let's talk about him.'

'I wish I understood your connection.'

'I'm your lucky charm. I'm better luck than you deserve,' said Sam.

'You don't belong to Harrigan,' said Winters slowly. 'I'm sure of that.'

'Good old Phil,' said Sam. 'I'd dance on his coffin.'

Winters had squared around in his seat so that he faced Sam. 'Were you at the hotel this evening by accident? I think it's time you gave me a few answers. You pretend to know a lot, but I wonder if you do.'

'I didn't start yesterday,' said Sam, 'I've been around.'

'Harrigan was the only one who knew what I was doing tonight,' said Winters, 'and he didn't put you on to me. So you're an outsider, whoever you are.'

'I'm giving you a nice free ride home,' said Sam.

'You puzzle me.' Winters shifted back in his seat and gazed at the road.

'You're the boy with his shirt hanging out, not me,' said Sam happily. 'Some time soon Phil will have to know what happened, how much are you going to tell him?'

'I'm thinking about it,' said Winters.

'I wish you luck,' said Sam, 'and I still think you're in the wrong line of business.'

They were now along the Ringwood road

and moving very smartly. Jerry Winters had lapsed into an uneasy silence, and Sam could well understand that he had many things on his mind, and none of them would be pleasant.

There was that nice wife of his for one thing. She would certainly give him an earful when he rolled in after midnight with that mess across his forehead. And then there was Phil Harrigan. He never tolerated any leakage in one of his undertakings, and if Winters started quoting how helpful a stranger had been – a stranger who had tailed him all the way without being noticed and who apparently knew Phil himself – Phil would blow his stack.

After long thought, Sam said, 'Can I give you some advice?'

'No,' said Winters.

'Well I hope you're a good liar,' said Sam, unabashed. 'You'll need to be when Phil gets after you. If he hears there was a third party with you he'll have your stripes and you know I'm not fooling. He can be a very rough man when things don't suit him.'

'I'm not worried,' said Winters.

'You ought to be,' said Sam. 'I see nothing but grief ahead of you.'

Winters replied that he could cope, but his tone and his general demeanour didn't suggest too much confidence.

'You're in over your head,' said Sam. 'You'd

be better off in jail – Phil mightn't get to you there.'

'You're being very clumsy and obvious,' said Winters. 'What you're really frightened of is that I might tell Harrigan about you.'

It was very near the truth, but Sam just grinned. 'Phil walked past me in the dining-room this evening, did you see him take any notice of me? Phil is a bright boy, and plenty of people know about him, so if you're crazy enough to tell him how I dug you out of the dirt tonight, you just mention that I might be putting in a few phone calls – I could drop a name to the police, for instance, and Phil wouldn't find that too convenient. Neither would you, boyo, would you? You get the point?'

Jerry Winters got it all right.

'I think you've said enough,' he said. 'I shouldn't have expected anything else.'

'I haven't finished,' said Sam. 'Don't forget there's the feller whose name you're being so shy about, he'll be interested, and I'll know in the morning who he is. He might like to have it confirmed by an eye-witness that Harrigan arranged the fire. There might even be a reward, they'll know it was arson, the blokes from the fire brigade couldn't miss it, and if you think I don't have the nerve to claim any reward that's going you don't know me.'

'I can believe that,' said Winters.

'You better believe it,' said Sam. 'Any time I have information worth selling, I usually find the market. So if you have to open your trap to Harrigan you can tell him that as well.'

It was after midnight when Sam stopped well short of the front of the hotel, and as Winters prepared to get out, Sam's parting words were, 'box clever and you might get away with it, and don't forget to have a good story about your car – it's an important detail ... pity about your face, if the night porter sees it he'll remember it, so slide in there fast. And hope he won't notice.'

'I'm not a complete fool,' said Winters stiffly. 'I know what I have to do.'

Sam's only comment was a soft laugh. He was wishing he could follow Winters inside for the next few minutes, particularly when he got upstairs and had to show himself to his wife.

Winters had got out of the car. He thrust his head in again and said rapidly, 'That name you're so interested in, it's Russell Colley – he's a Member of Parliament amongst other things, and he wouldn't pay you a reward, he'd have you arrested as an accessory ... good night.'

Sam watched him walk along the pavement and turn in at the hotel, the door wasn't locked, so perhaps he wouldn't have

121

to explain his face to the night porter or whoever was on duty. It would be different when his wife got hold of him. There were still cars parked on each side of the street, so it was just possible that Winters might make his story stick about having his car nicked in the night.

As he drove away Sam was reflecting on his own smartness in fixing that front tyre – it had helped to create a very promising situation, with Sam Harris pulling the strings. Nice. There had to be some way for him to cash in on what he knew. Somebody would pay him to keep his trap shut.

Phil Harrigan? Sam had a nasty cold shiver down the small of his back. That would take some smart handling all right. Phil wasn't an easy mark, putting the squeeze on him might be inviting real trouble.

In spite of that dirty crack from Winters, Sam thought the M.P. might be a better bet. He didn't know much about Members of Parliament, but he had heard of Russell Colley, most people had, because he was so often on the telly chat programmes. A very smooth performer with loads of charm, he had come to the front in recent years. Stacked with money, no doubt about that, and supposed to be a bit of a play-boy and sportsman, not just racing yachts, but breeding and racing horses as well–

Horses! That had to be it – that prosperous farm must have had racing stables, thoroughbreds worth thousands, and that clot Winters said he thought he'd been setting fire to an empty building! As if Phil Harrigan would bother with rubbish like that.

When Sam drove in past the front office at 'Ocean View' all was quiet and peaceful, and he wondered where Harry Harding was bedding down. There were no lights in any of the caravans. He prudently removed his capital from the boot of the car and took it into the caravan, and the comforting feel of that tidy packet of cash reminded him of what had not been in his mind for the last few hours because too much else had been happening.

He lay on his bed, smoking in the dark, and thinking about what had started back at *'Bernie's Place'*. From one of the caravans came the squalling of a baby in the night. The joys of parenthood had never been any part of Sam's scene, and he fell asleep while the baby was still in full cry. He'd had no sleep at all last night, and now it was after one.

He slept late and missed the news bulletin at nine. It was a bright sunny morning and the caravan smelt stuffy and stale, and the kids from the caravan next to his were out again and full of noisy activity with their yapping dog and the ball. The whole camp was on the go, out there in the sunshine; family parties getting ready for the seaside or trips to the New Forest; loads of kids.

Sam knew that people might start to get nosy if he spent too much time alone in his caravan with the curtains drawn. Single blokes didn't act like that – this was supposed to be a place where people came for a holiday.

He made himself some tea and toast, and made a mental note to get in some bottles of stuff before he spent another night there on his own. He didn't have to punish himself that much. A couple of good snorts might make up for not having a bird around.

There was a small shower cabinet, not enough room to turn around in even for a little skinny feller like himself, but it woke him up and brought back some of the old Harris bounce. He had a quick shave to finish off.

He put on one of the bright shirts he had acquired, and a spotted cravat tastefully knotted. He inspected himself in the mirror inside the little wardrobe door. He could pass for thirty-five, no trouble – this was no haunted fugitive. Debonair, that was it. Very sharp.

He transferred some more cash from the packet to his wallet and stuffed the packet back into his case. Then he saw Harry Harding cross the patch of grass and head his way. Hell. He couldn't pretend he was out.

Harding stopped and did the nice uncle bit with those two kids, jolly smiles and patting on the head and all that crap. He even gave their ball a boot to show what a sport he was.

He saw Sam through the tiny window and gave him a half-salute, so Sam opened the door and smiled a welcome he was far from feeling.

'Nice morning,' he said cheerily. 'I like your weather down here.'

'We get few complaints, Mr Foster,' said Harding, and Sam had to think before he remembered that he was Mr Foster from Cambridge.

'I trust you slept well, okay if I come in?'

'Be my guest,' said Sam, retreating to avoid being rammed by Harding's belly.

'Everything in order?' Harding seated himself without being invited, and glanced sharply round like a landlord taking an inventory.

'The telly doesn't work,' said Sam.

Harding clicked his tongue. 'It was all right when I left it, Mr Foster. I've always found it very reliable. However, if you let me have your key I'll have a man come in and fix it for you – that do?'

'Why not take it with you?' said Sam pleasantly. 'It's meant to be a portable.'

'I could do that,' said Harding. 'If you prefer it. You plan to be out for the day no doubt?'

'If it doesn't snow,' said Sam.

Harding obliged with a belly laugh, but his sharp eyes didn't join in. 'You have friends in this neighbourhood, Mr Foster?'

'Not yet,' said Sam.

'You'll find this something of a change after Cambridge,' said Harding.

'Yes.' So he was Mr Foster from Cambridge.

'You wouldn't be from the university, would you?'

'No,' said Sam promptly.

'I was only asking because sometimes we have students here during their vacations, holiday jobs, you know the kind of thing I mean, and I was wondering if you happened to know any of them.'

'It's a biggish place,' said Sam, and waited for Harding to come right out with it and ask him what he did for his bread.

'Well, I do hope you will enjoy your stay with us,' said Harding, getting up with obvious reluctance. 'If it interests you, I could arrange to get you accepted as a visiting member at one or two clubs around here. Quite select places, if you see what I mean.'

'Very kind of you,' Sam said. So Harding

gets a rake-off from the local knocking shops as well as all the rest. A very busy boy.

'I hope I'm not speaking out of turn,' said Harding, giving Sam a thoughtful look. 'You may have your own plans.'

'I'm easy,' said Sam. He could guess what was coming.

'The way I see it,' said Harding, 'if a gentleman finds himself on his own, and if he likes to spend a little money he might as well do it in pleasant company.'

'I couldn't agree more,' said Sam. No birds on the camp, but Harding had outside talent available.

Harding nodded. 'I rather thought you would, Mr Foster. I notice you don't keep very early hours.'

'I like to get about,' said Sam. 'Here and there.'

'Quite,' said Harding smoothly. 'It might become a little dull here for a man like yourself, and it did in fact occur to me that you might welcome a little entertainment.'

Sam grinned. 'I'm always open to any reasonable offer.'

'One has to be discreet about these things,' said Harding. 'But I'm sure I can arrange some introductions that won't disappoint you.'

Sam put on his cunning look. 'Sounds interesting all right – a little feminine company wouldn't be out of the way ... did I get you wrong?'

Harding's belly jumped up and down with heavy laughter. 'Precisely, Mr Foster. Any evening you feel yourself in the mood just give me the word and I'll see you right. It'll help to pass the time.'

'I never heard of a better way,' said Sam. 'Here, don't forget this.' He lifted the television set and dumped it in Harding's arms. 'I'll call in for it later, no hurry.'

He smiled into Harding's face, and Harding was unable to stop himself from looking a shade disgruntled at losing this excuse for visiting the caravan when Sam mightn't be there.

'I'll have it seen to,' he said, and took his departure.

Sam watched him waddle across the grass, the set clasped to his chest. Wouldn't you like to know what I was up to last night, and the night before, you fat ponce? Sam was thinking.

In the course of his career Sam had been engaged in a variety of unsavoury activities, as he would be the first to admit, but none of them had involved taking a percentage off a woman for her bedroom exploits with strangers. That was what Harding was after. He probably charged the client a fee as well for the introduction. A crude bastard.

Sam caught the next news bulletin on the

radio. There was nothing about the business at *'Bernie's Place'*, not a word. That might be good, then again it might be not so good. The fuzz would be digging away and they had plenty to keep them busy – two corpses, one of them with a slug in him – clear evidence of a bungled robbery by blokes who should have known what the were doing, and an anonymous tip-off on the phone.

Reflecting on it, Sam found himself beginning to sweat. He was thinking of the tricky bits again, like Percy being identified and Lily hearing about it.

They would have put a name on Percy by now. If they put it out over the air, or in the papers, and it reached Lily there wasn't a hope in hell that she would keep it to herself, not after the raw deal Sam had given her.

And there was nobody who could make up a better picture of Sam Harris than Lily. One of those identikit jobs. She knew every inch of him, the smart lover-boy who had ditched her.

Then, to add to his uneasiness, Sam remembered Dusty Miller. There was another one who could connect Sam with Percy, and he wouldn't for a minute hesitate to do it. Percy had introduced Sam as his partner, and Sam had done the paying for the cutting gear they had left behind at *'Bernie's Place'*, the gear Dusty Miler had been so anxious to get back because it might be traced back to him.

It might take the fuzz some time to get around to a dump like Dusty's, but it could happen, and Dusty wasn't going to keep his mouth shut for thirty-five quid. If they put any pressure on him, he'd give them a good working description of Sam Harris.

That made two angles to worry about. Sam had been on the run before, and he was by nature an optimistic character because he had often escaped personal disaster when the odds were against him. But this could be a very sticky one indeed, and he was feeling more than a little depressed as he listened to the rest of the news.

The item he had been expecting came up at the end: White Ford House was the name of the place where Jerry Winters had started the fire, on the Hampshire border; extensive damage had been done to farm buildings adjacent, and several valuable race horses had had to be destroyed. White Ford House was the property of Mr Russell Colley, the Member of Parliament and a prominent sportsman.

The White Ford stud was described as one of the most successful in the country in recent years, and Mr Russell Colley estimated that his losses in the fire to be many thousands of pounds. Only the prompt action of the staff had prevented the fire from spreading to the main building, and preliminary investigations indicated that the fire had been started in one of the stables deliberately.

Clearly the work of a criminal maniac, Russell Colley had pronounced. Police inquiries were proceeding...

Sam wondered if Jerry Winters and his wife had heard the broadcast, and he was willing to bet that Winters had got very little sleep that night. He was also willing to bet that Anne Winters had nagged the truth out of her husband somehow or other.

He couldn't spend the morning chewing his fingers in that little rabbit hutch and wondering just how lousy everything had become. His luck could still hold, couldn't it? He transferred his capital once more to the boot of the car, and set out.

EIGHT

Just outside the town he found a newspaper shop and bought a couple. Sitting in the car he couldn't stop himself flipping through both of them, and he came across only one short reference: they had labelled it *The Social Club Killing* ... police investigations had moved to the London area, and a number of clues were being followed up. Just that.

Sam drove down the main street in the sunshine. Everybody was out, and he couldn't find an empty space. He had to drive on down to near the water before he could leave the Viva.

There seemed to be even more boats out there than before, and he tried to pick out Phil Harrigan's cruiser, but he could see nothing like it anywhere around, nothing as big; most of the boats had sails, and quite a few of them were heading out down the channel.

He walked along as far as he could go without having to paddle, and he still couldn't spot the cruiser. According to Winters, Phil Harrigan wasn't due back in the place for a couple of days, but Winters had said he'd been allowed the use of the boat in the absence of the boss, so he had probably taken it out.

Sam strolled back up the hill to the hotel. The bar was open, they were serving coffee in the dining-room, and he caught a passing glimpse of his waitress, the friendly and observant Eileen. He walked in and found a table to himself – the one he'd been at the night before, so Eileen would be serving him.

When she came over with her little tray he gave her his most guileless smile.

'Lovely morning, Eileen,' he said. 'Coffee?'

'Would you like some biscuits or cakes with it?' She lowered her voice and brushed some crumbs off the table. 'I think he got drunk last night – they had an early breakfast and went out...'

'Biscuits,' said Sam. 'Thanks very much.'

When she brought the tray back she bent over him as she put the coffee down. 'They spent most of the night having a row, that's what it looked like when they came down for breakfast – he had a bump on his face...'

'Maybe she hit him with the wardrobe,' Sam murmured.

Eileen gurgled. 'Will that be all, sir?'

'To be going on with.' Sam gave her a fifty pence piece and told her to keep the change and she didn't argue, a nice sensible girl.

'She'd been crying, you could tell... I feel sorry for her myself...'

'Me too,' said Sam.

'She ought to leave him, I know I would.'

'You've got sense,' said Sam softly.

'Will you be in for lunch, sir? I could reserve this table if you like, we get rather crowded.'

'I'll have to skip it,' said Sam. 'Dinner maybe.'

If Jerry Winters had taken his wife out in the cruiser, which seemed likely, they'd be out all day, so there was no point in hanging around the hotel, doing the smart private eye bit – where would it get him?

He sipped his coffee, it was nothing special, just an excuse for being there. There was clearly nothing more to come from Eileen, she was standing at the end of the room, chatting with one of the girls. She had told him nothing that he couldn't have guessed for himself, except that Mr and Mrs Winters had had an early breakfast.

He collected his car and set out on the road he'd followed after Jerry Winters the night before. There was plenty of traffic and he was in no hurry.

He pulled up on the grass verge behind a couple of cars just in front of White Ford House. It seemed safe enough to add himself to the little group of sight-seers who had climbed the bank to stand and gawp at what they could see of the blackened ruins of the stables. There was much speculation about the value of the thoroughbreds that had perished in the fire – race horses had a special appeal, not like cows.

One knowledgeable character in a hacking jacket that showed he was a bit of an expert on horse-flesh reckoned that old Colley wouldn't get any change from a hundred thousand quid when everything was paid for even with the insurance, you could take his word for it.

'He'll likely lose that much in stud fees, see? I hear one of the horses they had to put down was *Colley's Lad* – the best stallion he had, if you ask me…'

The general opinion was that it was a wicked shame and something ought to be done about it bloody quick. White Ford House looked attractive in the sun; two storeys with a green tiled roof and plenty of windows all gleaming; not a working farmer's house – it was far too spacious and well kept, the kind of country house that would run to half a dozen bathrooms and a separate cottage for the staff.

Among the superior cars parked on the drive Sam noted the police car, and the uniformed driver talking to another chauffeur type in a black saloon. Russell Colley, Member of Parliament and wealthy patron of the Turf, had probably whipped in the Chief Constable himself to sort things out. Only the best would be good enough for him.

Jerry Winters had said the fire was part of a campaign, that there was some kind of a feud between Phil Harrigan and Russell Colley. If that was so, it had to mean that Mr Russell Colley, M.P. and all the rest of it, wasn't quite as white as the driven snow … otherwise he wouldn't be colliding with Phil Harrigan. There had to be some dirt there somewhere.

Last night, Sam reflected, I should have put some real pressure on Winters. I had him wobbling and I could have got the full story out of him. I must be going soft.

He got back into the car and drove on to where Jerry Winters had come to grief in the ditch. The Sprite had been salvaged; he could see the marks on the soft grass where the breakdown truck had run up to the edge of the ditch, and the splinters of glass that must have come from the Sprite's lights.

He had some food at a good quality place in the square at Wimborne where he had trouble finding a place to park, and early in the afternoon he was in a busy post office in Bournemouth. He looked up Russell Colley's number at White Ford House, and decided it would be crazy to put in the kind of call he had in mind while the fuzz might be still on the premises.

Colley would have other houses, his kind of bloke always did, but after what had happened the chances were that he might spend some time at White Ford House seeing to it that the underlings cleared things up, and so on.

Sam parked his car and walked down to the Pavilion and the gardens. He had never done a job in Bournemouth, but it certainly was a place loaded with cash, and talent. And not the kind of opposition you might come up against in Brighton, for instance. Not so many professional operators, maybe.

One of those plushy hotels would be just the place to pick up a rich widow who was missing it, and not too long in the tooth to be past it. Cocktail lounge stuff and a bit of style. It could happen.

When his plate wasn't quite so full he might give the possibility some attention. He sat on the promenade and surveyed the passing scene, a gentleman at leisure. The sun was shining and the sea was nearly blue, and pretty soon now it might be time to put in that call to Russell Colley and see how it developed. He had something that should have a good market price, unless he was very much wrong about Russell Colley.

Conning an M.P., now that was something new for Sam. Like putting the black on a bishop.

He watched the strolling birds and found most of them too young to interest him; just kids down for a bit of holiday fun. In safe pairs. Like Margate or Southend.

He saw one who took his fancy. She was no giggling teenager. She carried it all nicely packaged. Blonde, in a blue sun-bathing outfit. Drifting along alone. When she turned and came back he got up and followed, just for the practice. She had an interesting movement, professional, like a model, or a dancer; in the habit of showing herself off to the best advantage – and her legs were a knock-out. Winners all the way.

By the pier she was accosted by one of those beach photographers; she posed very expertly while he did his bit, and Sam imagined she was actually smiling at him. Then she switched the smile off, took her ticket and crossed briskly to the Pavilion gardens.

He hesitated, and when he followed he had lost her. Pity. But he did not abandon the chase, and he caught sight of her again in front of the Pavilion. She was waiting for a break in the traffic, and he fetched up smartly alongside. She was aware of him. She turned her head and looked clean through him. Ice-blue eyes. A crisp lady-like voice said, 'Do go away, little man, you irritate me.'

'My mistake,' said Sam. 'I thought I knew you.'

'Highly unlikely,' she said, very upper-class.

End of conversation. Sam beat her to the other side of the road and kept on walking. You have to lose sometimes.

Back to the call boxes at the post office. What he was going to do wouldn't please Phil Harrigan, but he wouldn't have to know about it. He dialled the White Ford House number, and he was remembering the call he'd put in the night before last – this would be one with cash on the end of it, and that made all the difference.

A man's voice answered.

'I'd like to talk to Mr Russell Colley,' Sam said. 'It's personal.'

'I'm afraid Mr Russell Colley is not available. Would you care to leave a message?'

'No,' said Sam.

'I'm sorry, but if you let me have your name, and a number where you can be reached–'

'That won't do either,' said Sam, very business-like. 'You mean he's not in the house?'

'He is not available at the moment.' The voice had become starchy. 'Will you kindly give me your name and state your business.'

'My business is with your boss, it's personal, like I told you, and it's urgent. If he's not there, where can I get in touch with him?'

'I must insist on knowing who you are before we take this any further.'

'So he's there,' said Sam. 'Put him on the line.'

'Mr Russell Colley is dining in London... I must tell you that he does not accept anonymous telephone calls. If you are unable to give me your name, there is nothing I can do for you, you must surely appreciate that.'

'My name wouldn't mean a thing, to you or your boss,' said Sam. 'I wouldn't go to all this trouble if it wasn't serious, would I?'

'I am unable to answer that. Men in public life are frequently pestered by cranks, and all of them imagine their affairs are terribly important ... now we really must end this conversation–'

'I wouldn't do that,' said Sam. 'I don't think your boss will like it when he hears–'

'Indeed?' Very snooty.

'You cut me off now and your face will be very red.'

The voice became a little smoother, amused, perhaps. 'My dear man, whoever you are, you mustn't think you can threaten me.'

'I just did,' said Sam. 'I'm not talking for the fun of it.'

'Do please listen to me sensibly. If you have a problem and you think Mr Russell Colley can help you, put it all down on paper and send it to his London office. I can give you the address or you can look it up in the book. If your case warrants it an interview may be arranged later.'

'That sounds nice,' said Sam. 'But what I want to talk to your boss about doesn't go down on paper.'

There was a pause. 'I'm afraid I don't quite understand you.'

'You don't have to,' said Sam.

'You really must make yourself clearer.'

'What are you?' said Sam. 'The butler or the head man in the stables?'

'I am Mr Russell Colley's private secretary.' It was said with some dignity.

'Must be a nice job,' said Sam. 'Is he spending the night in London or coming back? Would that be top-secret information?'

'You are being impertinent. My employer's movements can have nothing to do with you.'

'Listen,' said Sam. 'I have news for you – you are not doing your boss much good by acting the stuffed shirt with me, so give it a rest, boyo, and let's have a bit of cooperation.'

'I cannot imagine why I should listen to you any longer – you refuse to give your name or say what your business is, so there is little point in going on with this conversation.'

'I might try again later,' said Sam. 'Is he coming back? He'll want to hear what I can tell him.'

'You are becoming a nuisance–'

'I'm worse than that when I really try,' said Sam. 'Suppose I say I'll ring in the morning? Will he be with you?'

'Probably, but I must warn you that he does not accept anonymous calls–'

'He'll accept this one,' said Sam. 'Just tell him it's about horses, you got that?'

'Horses?'

'That's what I said,' Sam repeated. He had rung the bell there all right. 'I want to talk to your boss about horses.'

The voice laughed, a very superior and insulting laugh.

'You find that funny?' Sam demanded.

'My dear good fellow, you must be quite out of your mind if you imagine for one minute that Russell Colley has time to talk to racing touts or tipsters, the idea is too ridiculous!'

'Have a good laugh,' said Sam, 'then listen to *me:* I'm not tipping a horse–'

'I'm so relieved,' said the voice, very amused still. 'I didn't think even a racing tout would be so idiotic as to try and sell inside information to Mr Russell Colley ... now get off the line and don't bother us any more–'

'Dead horses,' said Sam. 'He'll be interested in dead horses–'

'What was that?' Very sharp and crisp now.

'You heard,' said Sam.

'You must make yourself clearer – I must have more details ... hullo, are you still there? What was that about dead horses?'

'Personal and private for Russell Colley himself,' said Sam. 'You tell him that.' And he rang off.

He thought he had handled it pretty neatly for a start. Just enough information to have them nibbling for more ... 'dead horses' – a touch of genius there.

He found a pub near the shopping arcade and bought a light ale; it was early and he was nearly the sole customer. He liked a pub to be full and noisy, with a bird or two decorating the place. He was getting just a little tired of his own company, and there wasn't going to be anybody in that plate-glass morgue worth talking to.

He could spend the evening in Bourne-mouth, find the right spot for some good food, and inspect what talent might be around – a bird with her own flat? Another one like Lily? He didn't care to think too much about Lily, and not because he was missing her as a bed-mate.

There was a copy of the local evening paper on the bar. Much of Sam's newspaper reading was done in pubs where free copies were provided, along with nuts and crisps. Routine perks for any drinker. And the barman could glare as much as he liked. Free-loading off a bar had kept Sam going during many a ribby period; in the London area he had made a science out of eating on the strength of one little beer.

The fire at White Ford House and stables was given good coverage, with pictures of the stables, and dramatic quotes from some of the staff who had been first on the scene. Russell Colley himself was shown standing in the impressive porch of the house, a commanding country gentleman in tweeds, who confessed himself shocked at such an outrage which had resulted in the loss of valuable thoroughbreds...

Sam could find nothing about 'Bernie's Place', and while the barman was at the other end of the bar Sam left with the paper folded under his arm. If Jerry Winters and his wife had spent the day out in Phil Harrigan's cruiser they might like to know the news. Like hell they would.

He sat in the Viva, and decided that he wasn't after all in the mood to steam around Bournemouth looking for a woman for the night. There'd be plenty of other nights and women were like buses – you miss one so you take another.

Jerry Winters now, Phil Harrigan's reluctant boy, how was he handling himself? There was a lad with a real problem. And Phil? Sam didn't think Phil was going to be too happy.

Sam wasn't at all anxious to meet Harrigan, but Lymington was the place for the action. If he could make contact with Jerry Winters and push hard at him he could get the story about Harrigan's rough business with Russell Colley, and that would give him more weight when he got through to Colley.

He had parked his car and was walking up the slope again to the hotel when he saw something that had him crossing the road to inspect the shop windows opposite. There was a police car outside the hotel, no driver. It was a few minutes after seven, and the pavements were not so crowded as in the morning.

With Sam it was automatic to keep well

clear when he spotted a police car. He lit a cigarette and dawdled along the street, pausing now and then, a dedicated window-shopper, passing the time on a fine summer evening.

In due course, after he had smoked two cigarettes and had given his best attention to gear he could never want to buy, he saw the constable come out of the hotel and get in the car; he was alone so it must have been some routine business, otherwise there would have been two of them. The car swept smartly up the street, past where Sam stood.

And then, out of the corner of his eye, Sam became aware that he was himself under observation, so very casually he shifted around. Anne Winters was partly hidden in the doorway of a closed shop; she wore jeans and a blue anorak, and her face was far from happy. She nodded and began to walk briskly up the street away from the hotel.

Sam overtook her, and without pausing or looking at her, he said, 'Trouble?'

'Yes,' she said. 'Is your car handy?'

'Keep walking,' he said. 'I'll pick you up.'

He turned and went back to where he had left the Viva, and he surprised himself by not giving it a second thought. He had his own trouble, and here he was jumping right into somebody else's mess. He did a saucy U-turn, and got rightly cursed by the driver of a car towing a trailer with a sailing boat who had to stop in a hurry on the slope.

With the minimum of delay Sam pulled up by Anne Winters and she slid in beside him and they were off.

'Thank you,' she said faintly. 'You saw that policeman?'

'We both saw him,' said Sam.

'He wanted Jerry.'

'I'm not surprised,' said Sam. He reached into the glove compartment and took out the folded newspaper and put it in her lap. 'It doesn't make a nice story,' he said.

'I know.' She didn't read the paper, just stared straight ahead, clutching the paper. 'Jerry told me everything ... he didn't know it would be like that – it was too late to stop the fire when he found there were horses in there ... it was horrible...'

'It was that all right,' said Sam. 'I was there – what did the police want?'

'It was about Jerry's car. I was with him when he reported that it had been stolen, and from what they asked him I don't think they believed him – we expected they'd be back.' She gave Sam a quick glance. 'I've been waiting and hoping I'd see you, Jerry was sure you'd be at the hotel some time, and that policeman arrived while I was waiting on the street.'

'You haven't been back to the hotel since you left early this morning.'

'I didn't dare,' she said.

146

'I'd emigrate if I were you,' said Sam drily. 'You've got Harrigan's cruiser, in a job like that you could go round the world. You've been out in it all day, right? If I had the coppers breathing down my neck – and probably Phil Harrigan as well – I don't reckon I'd hang around too long.'

She was silent for a moment. Then, 'What puzzles Jerry and me, is where you stand in this. You followed him last night, and you helped him when he needed help, and he says you know Harrigan, but you don't work for him ... most people would have told the police about last night.'

'So you can work that one out for yourself,' said Sam. 'But I'll tell you this much – the day I volunteer information to the police as a law-abiding citizen should is one hell of a long way off.'

'I see.'

'Don't need to be polite,' said Sam, 'not with me. I've done a bit of this, that, and the other. Nothing too drastic, understand? But not strictly legitimate, if you want to be fussy.'

'We're in no position to be fussy,' she said.

'You're in a jam all round,' said Sam.

She was quiet for so long that Sam thought she might be crying, and when he took a look at her he saw that tears were not far off. He didn't think Anne Winters would cry too easily, not like some birds he knew.

He passed her his case and said, 'Help yourself and do one for me.'

She fumbled the cigarette case open. 'I'm sorry,' she said. Her voice was uneven, but she wasn't going to cry. She lit the cigarettes, and as she passed him one she managed a small uncertain smile.

'You're a strange man,' she said slowly. 'Jerry didn't understand you, and neither do I ... you're very surprising.'

'I've heard plenty of people put it another way,' he said.

'We're completely in your hands, you know enough to get Jerry into serious trouble.'

'That husband of yours,' said Sam. 'You ought to knock some sense into him—'

'I will,' she said earnestly. 'After last night, there won't be any more ... he won't be working for Harrigan, I'll see to that! My husband isn't a criminal, whatever you think of him!'

The loyal little wife was saying her piece. Sam went on driving.

'You don't have to convince me,' he said. 'I'm just the driver – by the way, where are we heading?'

'Would you be willing to help us?'

'If your husband intends to duck away from Phil Harrigan he's going to need more help than I can give him,' said Sam.

'I see,' she said. 'It was rather too much to expect. Jerry said you wouldn't agree, but I said I'd try – we owe you more than enough already. Would you please drop me somewhere so that I can catch a bus … then we won't bother you any more.'

'I'm giving you a ride,' said Sam. 'That doesn't pledge me to anything, right? And I haven't seen a bus-stop anywhere along here.'

'I could hitch-hike,' she said.

'You might never get there wherever it is,' said Sam. 'Believe it or not, you're safer with me.'

'I don't know why, but I believe I am.'

'Thanks a million,' said Sam. 'It must be my honest face. I'll drive you where you want to go, but that doesn't mean I'm ready to get tangled up with Phil Harrigan. Agreed?'

'Yes,' she said.

'So give me a few clues,' said Sam. 'I'm listening.'

NINE

'Jerry wants to talk to you,' she said. 'He wanted to come himself and find you, but I persuaded him it would be safer if I came instead, I'm not the one the police might be looking for about the car, and I knew I could keep out of the way… I was there nearly an

149

hour waiting for you. I saw the policeman arrive. I was in the café just across the street most of the time and I'd just come out when he stopped at the hotel, so I just walked up and waited, and you came... Jerry has some information he thinks you might like to know.'

'A proposition?' said Sam. 'It'll have to be a good one.'

'He thinks it is, that's why I came to find you,' she said. 'You know we took Harrigan's cruiser out this morning. We talked about it most of the night, and it seemed our best way out – we could get clear of Harrigan, and then in the morning it was obvious the police might ask more questions about Jerry's car, difficult questions that Jerry couldn't answer. We decided we'd go to Eire. I have some cousins farming near Waterford, and an uncle in Dublin. We would have been all right, and the weather forecast couldn't have been better–'

'So what went wrong?' said Sam. 'Hell, in that cruiser you could have aimed at Africa, never mind round the corner to Eire–'

'Jerry didn't check the fuel tanks,' she said flatly. 'We were in such a hurry to start, it wasn't easy for him, handling a boat that size on his own, I don't know anything about them so I wasn't much use ... but we should have noticed how little fuel there was...'

Sam was reflecting that when Jerry Winters loused a job up he did it in a big way.

'You ran dry,' he said.

'We did. I could have wept. We were miles out when the engines stopped and we just drifted for a couple of hours, trying to attract attention, waving clothes and so on, there were some boats but they didn't seem to notice, then a fishing boat came along and towed us in to Poole harbour ... we were lucky they spotted us. It frightened me, I must admit.'

'End of sea trip,' said Sam. 'It would have scared me rigid. So the boat's at Poole.'

'There was the question of insurance and the towing fee or salvage or whatever it was, it didn't belong to us, but Jerry managed to convince them that we hadn't stolen the boat. He had to give them Harrigan's name and his London address, that was unavoidable, and while they were checking they let us go for a cup of coffee, it was all quite friendly ... and we didn't go back, we just got on the first bus that came along.'

'There wasn't much else you could do,' said Sam. 'They wouldn't have let you take the boat out without the okay from Harrigan, and Phil would certainly want to know what the hell your husband was doing out there with no fuel in the tanks – that boat's worth a packet and Phil won't like paying any towing fee or whatever, he'll be on the way down to Poole right now.'

'We gathered that,' she said.

'So you want to vacate the neighbourhood fast?' said Sam. 'Is that where I come in?'

'There are regular flights to Dublin from the airport near Bristol,' she said. 'We could be on one in the morning. If Jerry hadn't smashed his car last night we would have driven to Bristol today, we might have been in Dublin by now.'

'Very snug,' said Sam.

'You're wondering what you get out of it,' she said.

'The idea had sort of crossed my mind,' he said. 'On general principles I think you're wise to get as far from Phil Harrigan as you can.'

'You mean you'll help us if it's worth your while? I think you should listen to what Jerry can tell you ... you have an interest in Harrigan, haven't you?'

'A very cautious one,' said Sam. 'Where do we meet your husband?'

It was a roadhouse on the Wimborne road, and Jerry Winters looked understandably relieved to see the two of them. He darted a quick glance at his wife, and she murmured, 'I think it will be all right.'

Sam nodded at him and said softly, 'You're a hell of a seaman – don't you know anything?'

'Not much,' said Winters.

There was plenty of business, but he had kept them a table in the restaurant away from the bar. While Anne Winters was away at the cloakroom, Sam said, 'that's a smart wife you have – you ought to look after her better.'

'Don't rub it in,' said Winters.

'I ought to have my head examined,' said Sam, 'listening to you after the dud performances you put up – so you want to skip the country–'

'Wouldn't you?' said Winters.

'You should have done it months ago, that would have been the smart move. What's the connection between Phil Harrigan and this Russell Colley bloke?'

'Money,' said Winters. 'Big money. Corruption and intimidation of public officials, fiddled contracts, payments under the counter–'

Anne Winters returned. A waitress arrived. She said the mixed grill was the best she could suggest. They ordered and Jerry Winters asked her to hurry it along because they didn't have much time.

When the girl had gone, Winters said, 'I don't have all the details, but I know enough, more than enough – and I have a pretty good idea of the sums of money involved. You apparently know Phil Harrigan and the way he operates – he's educated and intelligent, and a complete rogue.'

'Couldn't have put it better myself,' said Sam. 'He's a number one twister all through. Very sharp. Thinks big.'

'I think he's an unprincipled swine,' said Anne Winters very calmly.

'That makes it unanimous.' Sam grinned across the table at her, and then at her husband. 'Phil Harrigan is bad news. No fooling. And the other bloke? What's with him?'

'He's been running in double harness with Harrigan,' said Winters. 'Russell Colley is not the upright man he appears to be, and the skeleton in his particular cupboard is his association with a man like Harrigan. I don't quite know when or how it began, that was before Harrigan picked me up and gave me a job.'

Anne Winters made a disgusted sound. The waitress came with the food. Sam said he could manage a light ale, the other two weren't drinking. It was not a festive occasion. Anne Winters pushed her food about without much interest and crumbled a bread roll.

'I think Russell Colley is a bigger rogue than Harrigan,' she said. 'He's a hypocrite as well, trading on his public position, lining his own pockets – I've listened to him on television, so bluff and honest and caring for the welfare of the people! He ought to be exposed!'

'He's built himself into a public figure,' said Winters. 'He's got himself on to all sorts of committees, and he never misses a chance to advertise himself – and he does it very effectively, you have to grant him that. He puts himself across on television, for instance. He never tries to be too clever or theoretical, he leaves that to the professional economists who bore the pants off most of us.'

'He sounds like a right smart bastard to me,' said Sam.

'He's a public fake,' said Anne Winters succinctly. 'Tell him, Jerry.'

'He's created a public image for himself as a sort of John Bull politician who never fears to speak his mind, and somehow he seems able to guess which way the wind is going to blow,' said Winters. 'He's one of the few men in public life who might be recognised on the street. I met him twice, with Harrigan, and I found him charming on the surface – if I hadn't known something of the truth about him I would have said he was sincere and genuine. He was originally a lawyer, and a good one, from what I hear, so he knows how to cover his tracks. But somewhere along the line he cut a few fast corners. He didn't have much money behind him to start with, but now he's a comparatively wealthy man, and some of his money is just a little bit dirty if you look at it too closely. That's where Phil Harrigan comes in – Colley has been clever, but not quite clever enough. Most of us would like to think there isn't much corruption in public life today, but there are still openings for a dishonest man to make a private profit out of his public position.'

'Dodgy,' said Sam. 'With a feller like Phil breathing down your neck, that's asking for trouble.'

'I found out about it by accident,' said Winters. 'I happened to come across some interesting items on a bank statement that I wasn't supposed to see. So I did a little research. It took me some weeks before I began to put the picture together. The payments were made by companies in which Russell Colley had an interest – dummy companies that were being used as a cover. The cheques were made payable to Universal Enterprises – a label Harrigan uses. I'm not supposed to know about it. I've been employed to doctor his main accounts – he has money in shop properties that produce a legitimate income, and some other investments not so legitimate, but Universal Enterprises he keeps to himself.'

'Phil Harrigan on the fiddle with a rich M.P., that sounds juicy,' said Sam. 'Russell Colley wouldn't want that spread around.'

Winters took out his wallet. 'I'm not offering you money,' he said.

Sam grinned. 'It wouldn't insult me.'

156

'I can give you something that you might care to turn into cash,' said Winters. 'I have a cancelled cheque endorsed by Harrigan – it took some hard snooping before I got it, and I wouldn't like to be available when Harrigan finds out. The cheque is for five hundred pounds, payable to Universal Enterprises, and drawn by Domestic Developments and Company – one of Colley's dummy concerns. I think Russell Colley would be very unhappy to hear that the cheque had got into the wrong hands.'

'Like mine?' said Sam, quite cheerfully.

'It's blackmail,' said Anne Winters quietly.

'It's not nice,' Sam agreed. 'I've never tried it, but it's got possibilities, and these aren't nice people. I wouldn't lose any sleep over it, and that's the truth. You want something in return, right?'

'Transport,' said Winters. 'You have a car and it's too late for us to hope to hire one around here now. I've checked on the train service, it's no use to us at this time of the night. A car is the only answer.'

'You'd like a lift across to Bristol,' said Sam. 'Your wife gave me the hint on the way here.'

'Transport in return for information you may be able to use,' said Winters diffidently.

Anne Winters was watching Sam with special intentness, and he suddenly found it important to forget for once in his life that

157

he was Sam Harris, the smart boy who looked out exclusively for Number One.

He had on a number of occasions promised himself that he would never again stick his neck out just because a pretty girl had needed help – and this one had her husband with her as well.

'It could be done,' he said.

'Thank you,' said Anne Winters quietly. 'We don't even know your name yet–'

'Sam Harris.'

Winters slid the folded cheque across the table. 'If Russell Colley knows you've got it he will be nervous – you should be careful.'

Sam tucked the cheque away in his wallet. 'I'm careful,' he said. 'What really gives me the shakes is the thought of Phil Harrigan finding out.'

'A sensitive area,' Winters said. 'As far as I have been able to discover, Harrigan and Russell Colley had a serious disagreement recently. I gather Colley felt Harrigan had been milking him long enough. I overheard some angry telephone conversations that I wasn't meant to hear.'

'Phil Harrigan reckoned he had a soft income for life,' said Sam. 'He wouldn't kiss that good-bye without stirring up something.'

'Russell Colley took delivery of a new car,' said Winters. 'A Rolls-Royce. It was stolen from outside his London home the very first evening. When they found it in a quarry near Chester it was a complete wreck. And Colley didn't dare tell the police the true story. He can't afford to have his connection with Harrigan made public. There were other episodes that I can only guess at, but I know Harrigan arranged the Rolls-Royce business – it was a sample of the kind of harassment Colley could expect–'

'And then you set fire to his stables,' said Sam. 'So Phil Harrigan was stepping up the treatment, and he found a mug like you to do it.'

'Yes,' said Winters simply. 'I've told you how it happened, that was the truth... I didn't intend to do any harm to the horses, just the buildings – Russell Colley was very proud of his stables, it was meant to hit him where it would hurt, and remind him that Harrigan was still around.'

'Pretty crude,' said Sam. 'I wonder what else Harrigan has got up his sleeve? He could send a couple of his strong boys to give Colley a working over.'

'He won't do that yet,' said Winters.

'It'll happen,' said Sam. 'Colley might find it healthier and cheaper in the end to keep up the payments, after all, he can't call in the coppers, so he'll just have to go on taking it on the button when Harrigan dishes it out.'

'As far as I know,' said Winters, 'the cheque

I gave you is the last Harrigan received.'

Sam was again acutely conscious of Anne Winters' gaze. It might impress her if he whipped that cheque out and tore it up then and there. A bloody expensive gesture.

'What would really snarl it up,' he said, 'would be if a third party intervened and exposed both of them.'

'Mr Harris,' said Anne Winters, 'I think my husband and I would like to be across the water before anything like that happened.'

'I'm just thinking aloud,' said Sam. 'Phil Harrigan is a high-powered crook, and Russell Colley is a wealthy fake – remember the Poulson case? They got five years each. Once those Fraud Squad boys start digging they don't let up.'

'Jerry wouldn't have to appear, would he?' Anne Winters said. 'I mean as witness?'

'Perhaps not,' said Sam. 'You never can tell with courts.'

'I'm ready to take my chance on that,' said Winters.

'If they got their hooks solidly into Harrigan and Russell Colley they mightn't bother too much about the small fry, and that's all you were – you found out things you didn't have to know,' said Sam. 'Maybe I'll find I don't have the nerve to get it started, I'll have to give it some heavy thought when I've got rid of you two. You've probably guessed that I don't mix a lot with the fuzz.'

Anne Winters gave him a strained smile. 'I'll be happy to write you a character reference any time you need one, Mr Harris.'

Sam put on his boyish grin. 'It's time we did some travelling. We might make Bristol by eleven. Have you got somewhere to stay the night?'

'I know Bristol,' said Winters. 'While I was waiting for you I put in a call to a hotel I know, they're keeping a room for us, they could probably fit you in as well if you'd like to spend the night.'

'No thanks,' said Sam. 'It doesn't suit my plans.'

'I wish we knew more about you,' said Anne Winters, getting to her feet. 'You're still very much a mystery, Mr Harris.'

'Lot of people who know me wouldn't put it so politely,' said Sam. 'There's no mystery about me, I just scratch for my bread here and there.'

'I'm sure you don't do yourself justice,' she said with some warmth.

Justice. Hell, if only she knew the truth. 'Don't get any wrong ideas,' said Sam. 'I'm no guardian angel.'

She smiled. 'That might be open to argument, Sam Harris.'

The waitress arrived with the bill and Sam let Winters settle it. There was a service station attached to the restaurant, and Sam had the Viva loaded with five-star petrol for which Winters paid as well, which was only right and proper. There was no luggage, but Winters said it would be all right because he had told them at the hotel that he and his wife had been called away unexpectedly to visit a sick relative and would only be stopping one night.

Anne Winters sat in the back. Jerry Winters reckoned he knew the best cross-country route, and Sam proceeded to put up a very creditable performance. There was the minimum of conversation, and after a while Anne Winters appeared to be asleep.

'Listen,' said Sam softly, 'when you get over there, you mind you stay put and keep your nose clean – dig the potatoes, clean out the goddam pigs – but don't get yourself into any more fiddles. Am I right?'

'You're right,' said Winters, and his voice was very subdued.

'Easy money looks okay,' said Sam, 'but there's always strings attached. Believe me, boyo, I know. It takes a special temperament, and you don't have it. Phil Harrigan will be looking for you – you're defecting, and he won't like that. For one thing, you have inside information about the way he runs things–'

'Not much,' said Winters, 'but enough to know that for him crime pays very well indeed, and I don't mean just defrauding the Inland Revenue, plenty of people who consider themselves honest go in for that. It's like smuggling stuff through the Customs, almost respectable. I know Harrigan finances criminal enterprises, but I could never prove it. Have you decided what you will do with that cheque?'

'Not yet,' said Sam. 'You gave it to me, I didn't ask for it, remember.'

'It's dangerous,' said Winters. 'I wouldn't like you to get into any trouble about it, not after the help you've been to us.'

'You cope with your own grief,' said Sam. 'You've got plenty at risk – like a nice kind of a wife for instance. Try giving her a square deal for a change. It can't be much of a bargain for a decent girl like her, being married to a sloppy crook like you. She's worth something better than that.'

'I know it,' said Winters.

'So maybe you came unstuck in South Africa and got caught with your hand in the till,' said Sam. 'But what the hell, that doesn't mean you have to mess up the rest of your life with the likes of Phil Harrigan.'

'I know that as well,' said Winters.

'So do something about it,' said Sam. 'You've left it bloody late, but not too late if you use your loaf from now on.'

Here endeth the sermon and I am in no position to be preaching at anybody, Sam reflected.

'You're absolutely right,' said Winters quietly.

'Damn right I'm right.'

'I hope we can meet again sometime,' said Winters. 'Perhaps in rather better circumstances. I can let you have an address where we can be reached.'

'I wouldn't do that,' said Sam. 'I might take you up on it. You'd better chalk all this up to experience – and reckon yourself lucky you got out in time.'

'And what about you?' said Winters. 'You've been giving me excellent advice, you couldn't have been a greater help–'

'Let's leave it at that.' Sam's voice was crisp and business-like. 'I just happened to be around, that's all. Don't make a meal of it.'

'I'm sorry,' said Winters. 'I didn't mean to pry–'

'So skip it,' said Sam.

It was a few minutes after eleven when they stopped outside a small hotel near the Suspension Bridge in the Clifton district of Bristol.

'I'll just check that it's all right,' said Winters and got out of the car.

Anne Winters waited, then shifted forward in her seat, her hand touching Sam's shoulder. 'I heard most of what you've been saying to Jerry,' she said. 'I haven't really been asleep all the way, and I want to tell you this, Sam: I think you're a pretty good sort of man, no matter what you think of yourself ... or whatever you're doing – you've been hinting that you're some kind of a crook, and maybe you are – but you talked better sense to Jerry than I've heard from anybody for a long time.'

'I've just been talking,' said Sam. 'It costs nothing.'

'It sounded right to me,' she said, then leaning forward quickly, she kissed him very carefully.

'You're not so bad yourself,' he said.

'I'll remember you, Sam Harris,' she said softly, 'and I wish you the best of luck.'

'You too,' said Sam. 'Make him toe the line, and have a good trip.'

Jerry Winters had come out of the hotel and it was evident from his face that he had come across no snags.

'They don't have a liquor licence,' he said, 'but they can rustle up some coffee and sandwiches – are you interested, Mr Harris?'

'No thanks,' said Sam. He didn't think he could improve on the farewell Anne Winters had already given him, and there was nothing more he wanted to say to Jerry Winters. Anne Winters had got out and she was standing with her hand tucked under her husband's arm.

'Mind how you go, the pair of you,' said

Sam. 'It's a wicked world–'

And he drove off, leaving them there on the pavement. It was, he thought, a pretty effective exit. Sam Harris, the knight in shining armour, streaking off alone into the night.

The roads were fairly empty and he was now in no hurry. In the morning he might make that phone call to Russell Colley, and he would have something more to talk about than dead horses. Such as a dodgy cheque for five hundred smackers. Russell Colley wouldn't like that little bit of paper to be floating around, and if he got stroppy Sam could always suggest sending the cheque to the bright boys at the Fraud Squad with a few hints, anonymously of course. It should be fire-proof.

He turned it over in his mind as he drove through the countryside, and he liked it more and more. He wouldn't be risking anything as long as he boxed clever, and he told himself that he would box very clever indeed.

Putting the good old squeeze on a Member of Parliament, that would be a big enough deal for anyone, anyone like Phil Harrigan for instance. For Sam Harris it had to be the big winner. When Mister Russell Bleeding Colley heard what Sam had he wouldn't shout for the coppers. He would start sweating, and that was surely going to pay Sam a nice dividend.

He parked the Viva and collected the bundle from the boot before he let himself into the caravan. It was twenty-five minutes past one, and he seemed to be the only one on the site not asleep. That made three late nights in a row, so he had the right to be feeling tired.

He had climbed into his pyjamas when he noticed that the television set was back in its place. So that nosy Harry Harding had been snooping around. The nerve of the bloke. It would never do to leave that cash behind even for a couple of hours.

Sam climbed into his bunk and decided that he would have to find somewhere else pretty soon. This was too tricky all round. You couldn't trust anybody. He hoped Jerry Winters and his wife would get their plane in the morning. For a very little while he speculated about Phil Harrigan. Not a reposeful topic. So he gave it up and went to sleep.

TEN

There was a call box on the camp site next to the store, but Sam decided to try elsewhere because Harry Harding was standing outside the box talking to a woman who carried a loaded shopping basket, and there was a man making a call. So if he stopped and joined the queue he would have to put up with some funny cracks from Harding about the late hours he kept.

Harry Harding spotted him as he slowed and gave him a matey grin and a wave. Sam nodded and went on driving. He had listened again to the ten o'clock news broadcast, and he had heard nothing that even remotely pointed a finger in his direction, which was the right way to start the day.

From a call box in the town he rang White Ford House, and the same superior voice answered him as before and invited him to state his business.

'Just like yesterday evening,' said Sam. 'Dead horses. Is Russell Colley there?'

There was a pause, then another fruity voice came on: 'This is Russell Colley. I don't take anonymous calls – who are you?'

'You're taking this one,' said Sam.

'Explain yourself.'

'I've given you the clue,' said Sam. 'Some of your valuable horses are dead, and we both know who was responsible.'

There was another pause, longer this time.

'And we both know why,' Sam added.

'I see. Are you by any chance speaking for him?'

'Don't be daft,' said Sam.

'He knows I will not be intimidated.' Russell Colley's voice had little of the ring of confidence. 'Before we go any further you must clarify your position.'

'I'm the man in the middle,' said Sam. 'I'm pulling the strings on this one, and if you're thinking of trying to trace this call you'll be wasting your time.'

'You must as least tell me your name if you wish me to listen to you.'

'I'll tell you a name you'd like to forget about only he won't let you,' said Sam. 'Phil Harrigan.'

'If you happen to be in touch with him,' said Russell Colley very slowly, like a man feeling his way in the dark, 'you must know that I have made my position very clear to him, and that I cannot afford to continue–'

'You can't afford to stop,' said Sam. 'The next time it won't be your stables and horses, or your Rolls-Royce. You've upset him.'

'A glimpse of the obvious,' said Russell Colley. 'I may seem obtuse, but just why are you calling me? You have told me nothing I don't already know.'

'If you've got anybody listening in on this line you'd better get rid of them in your own interest,' said Sam.

'I am not altogether stupid.' Russell Colley's voice had gone quiet. 'I still fail to understand where you come into this. If you are not from Harrigan, then whom do you represent?'

'Just me,' said Sam.

'Tell me what you want.'

'I have something that could blow you sky high,' said Sam.

'So?'

'You wouldn't like to go to jail for corrupt practices, would you? I have a cheque for five hundred quid that can be traced back to you.'

Russell Colley cleared his throat. 'That is not possible. I do not believe it.'

'You've been asking me for names,' said Sam. 'Okay, try these two for size – Universal Enterprises, and Domestic Developments – that grabs you where it hurts, right, Mister M.P? That rings a few alarm bells. Shall I translate the names for you?'

The pause this time was a lengthy one, but Sam knew the connection hadn't been broken, and he was wishing he could see Russell Colley's face. He lit a cigarette and waited.

'This cheque you say you have,' said Russell Colley, 'how did it come into your possession?'

'People get careless,' said Sam. 'You know how it is.'

'I wonder if I do. Could it be that you are a thief?'

Sam laughed. 'Look who's talking. You've had your hand in the public till for years, you and your mate Phil Harrigan.'

'These are foolish allegations. Suppose I tell you that you cannot hope to substantiate them?'

'Don't give me that,' said Sam. 'I bet you're sweating all over the place in case I'm an honest citizen. I mean, all I have to do is send the cheque to the Fraud Squad with a few helpful clues, and that will start another stink in high places – you won't exactly come up smelling of violets, not once the Fraud boys start on you. And I'll tell you something else – Phil Harrigan will take off fast for foreign parts, Brazil or what-have-you, as soon as he sniffs trouble ahead. You'll carry the can all by yourself. They'll give you five years, I shouldn't wonder. So how do you like the sound of all that?'

'Not pleasant. Do you happen to have access to other cheques of a similar nature?'

'This one's enough for a start,' said Sam. 'Are you bidding?'

'I should have expected as much,' said

171

Russell Colley. 'Does Harrigan know you have that cheque?'

'You'd better ask him,' said Sam. 'He'll tell you to get knotted. You're the public figure with plenty to lose. Phil is a smart crook, you should know that. He won't hang around to be questioned.'

'He didn't put you up to this?'

'Ask him that as well,' said Sam. 'Are we in business?'

'I think we must meet, very soon,' said Russell Colley.

'Make me an offer,' said Sam.

'I would prefer to see you first, it would be to our mutual benefit. It is a delicate position.'

'You bet it is,' said Sam, 'which is why I don't intend to fiddle around with you any longer. Do we have a deal or do I send the cheque where it'll do you plenty of damage?'

'How much do you have in mind?'

'Twice the face value of the cheque,' said Sam. 'A thousand.'

'Ridiculous,' said Russell Colley promptly. 'You cannot be serious.'

'I'm serious,' said Sam just as promptly. 'You know bloody well I am.'

'I must have time to consider this–'

'You have fifteen seconds, starting now – and you'd better believe that I don't make jokes about money. I want a thousand quid, made up in fivers.'

'You are being extortionate. I would need time to have that amount available.'

'You'll hardly miss it,' said Sam, 'and you'll be saving yourself a lot of grief – I'm offering you a bargain.'

'I think five hundred would be a fair price,' said Russell Colley and Sam knew that he was home and dried.

'I must know how that cheque came to be in your possession,' said Russell Colley. 'I am concerned about others that you may have.'

'Let's concentrate on this one,' said Sam. 'Make up your mind, sport.'

'I am considering the implications.'

'A thousand quid,' said Sam, 'and you won't be hearing from me again.'

'My dear man, whoever you are,' said Russell Colley bitterly, 'that is the last thing I can believe – you intend to bleed me, I know that.'

'Listen,' said Sam, 'if I had more than one cheque I'd be squeezing you for a damn sight more than a thousand, you got my solemn word for that. You'll have to draw the money in London, correct? How many dodgy accounts do you keep up there? Half a dozen?'

'Let us confine ourselves to the matter in hand,' said Russell Colley stiffly, as though Sam had been guilty of a gross vulgarity. 'I can get the money in London.'

'Just don't try to be smart,' said Sam. 'Don't get it all from the same bank, then nobody will start getting inquisitive, like taking a note of the numbers of the fivers –I'm a nervous character.'

'Indeed? I hadn't noticed. Where do I meet you? I am due to be in London this afternoon and this evening. I will have the money ready by the time the banks close.'

'I'll ring you at your London address,' said Sam, 'and tell you what you have to do.'

'Not at my home address,' said Russell Colley. 'That will not be necessary, and I will not allow it.'

'You hope to keep the family background all nice and clean,' said Sam. 'They've got a shock coming – you picked the wrong bloke when you got tangled up with Phil Harrigan.'

'I have a business address in Sloane Street. It will be more convenient for me to use it. You will find it listed under Domestic Developments. May I suggest you make your call in the evening, then I can be sure of being alone in the office?'

'Half past seven,' said Sam.

'That would be convenient. Will you come to Sloane Street?'

'Is it likely?' said Sam. 'You could stuff the place with rough boys and have me jumped on.'

'You judge me by your own standards. Such an idea would never cross my mind.'

Sam laughed. 'I'm just protecting myself. You're a tricky bastard. You have the money ready and be sitting by the phone at half seven, then I'll tell you how we're going to do it.'

'You will have the cheque with you?'

'I will. But just in case you're thinking of arranging something for me,' said Sam, 'I'll do a little arranging myself.'

'I don't follow you,' said Russell Colley.

'You will, boyo, you will,' said Sam. 'There's a mate of mine, he'll have a couple of letters to post tonight if anything happens tonight that I don't fancy ... you getting the idea?'

'You don't trust me, is that it?' said Russell Colley with more dignity than a man in his position would normally assume.

'Trust you?' said Sam. 'Listen, I wouldn't give you my vote to save the country from a red revolution. You're a twister all the way down the line.'

'Abuse will get us nowhere,' said Russell Colley.

'I'll tell you what's in the letters,' said Sam. 'One for the experts at Scotland Yard, and the other goes to a newspaper that loves stirring up a public scandal – they'll have details of the cheque which the bank will be forced to disclose to the police, plus a few bits of information. So you'd better forget any ideas about bringing in some private muscle.'

'I have told you I have no such intention,' said Russell Colley, now almost pleading and not at all dignified. 'You add a needless complication.'

'I call it insurance,' said Sam. 'You didn't think I wouldn't protect myself, did you?'

'I take your point,' said Russell Colley.

'You can't do much else,' said Sam. 'Don't upset me or I can turn very nasty.'

'I will be completely alone this evening,' said Russell Colley. 'I will do whatever you wish. You will have no reason not to be satisfied.'

'You'll be hearing from me,' said Sam, and rang off. That was a neat stroke, that bit about the letters; now Russell Colley couldn't afford to try any clever stuff. What a pity Jerry Winters hadn't been able to snaffle a few more cheques. Colley was loaded and he was in a jam, so he would have paid up without a squawk.

Sam drove down through the town and parked near the water. Phil Harrigan's cruiser wasn't there, of course; they'd be holding it at Poole, arguing the toss about the legal rights and wrongs... Sam knew little about salvage but he hoped they had stung Harrigan good and hard.

When he strolled back up the hill he was keeping a very sharp eye for the kind of special vehicle Phil Harrigan would have – something big and expensive and fast, but he saw nothing that looked likely. He even went under the arch where the sign said: *Car Park. Hotel Patrons Only.* There was a selection of saloons, mostly family jobs, and a couple of vans, none of them good enough for Phil Harrigan. Harrigan hadn't recognised him two nights ago when he came in to talk to Jerry Winters, so Sam didn't feel he was taking any risk as he went into the hotel for a coffee.

He was early, and he was the only customer. Eileen came across to his table, and she was looking excited.

'Morning, Eileen,' he said. 'Coffee, I think.'

She glanced towards the glass door into the hall. 'We've had some drama,' she said quietly. 'It's Mr and Mrs Winters – they didn't come back last night, and nobody knows where they are, they didn't take any luggage, it's all in their room – and that Harrigan man, the one with the beard, he came last night and he was looking for them as well … you should have been here!'

'Glad I wasn't,' said Sam, grinning

'He was livid,' said Eileen with relish.

'I hope he's gone,' said Sam.

'Last night,' said Eileen. 'But that isn't all of it – we've got the police again, one of them is still here … asking about the Winters – we've all been questioned. I'm sorry, but I had to tell the detectives about you – I couldn't get out of it.'

She glanced over her shoulder. 'Some of the girls have noticed me talking in here to you, like now, and one of them told the detective I had a new boy-friend, she meant it as a joke of course, but he started asking me questions and I'm afraid it sort of came out – I told him I thought you knew the Winters. I'm sorry. I hope I haven't got you into any trouble?'

Sam shrugged. 'Not your fault.'

'I just blurted it out,' she said. 'I don't know your name but I gave him a description of you – I really couldn't do anything else.'

'I know how it is with coppers,' said Sam. 'I don't blame you.'

'Everybody's making such a fuss about the Winters,' she said. 'I can't believe they're criminals – but nobody seems to know just why they left.'

'Maybe they got tired of the cooking here,' said Sam. 'You say there's a copper still on the premises?'

She nodded.

Sam got to his feet. 'Skip the coffee,' he said. 'You haven't seen me this morning, right?'

Eileen was staring unhappily at the door into the hall. 'He's coming in,' she whispered.

A young man in a tweed jacket came in

from the hall and advanced towards them in a purposeful manner, and he had the healthy look of a man who likes his work, which made Sam's insides jump around because some of the young fellers who might be new to the job took some shaking off. With an old sweat of a copper you knew how far you could go.

'Ah, Eileen, in this the gentleman you mentioned?'

'Yes,' said Eileen in a small voice.

Sam had wisely subsided into his seat. There was nothing else he could do, and he was desperately wishing there had been time to find out just what Eileen had told the fuzz so that he could adjust his version accordingly.

The detective addressed himself to Sam: 'You won't mind if I have a few words with you, sir.' And it wasn't a question.

'Help yourself,' said Sam.

'I am Detective Constable Parker.'

Sam pretended to glance at the warrant card offered to him with mild surprise as though he had never seen one before which was not the case.

'What's the trouble, officer?' A nice manly start. The citizen with nothing to hide.

'One moment, sir, if you please,' said D.C. Parker, and smiled at Eileen. 'We'll have a couple of coffees, I think – that okay with you, sir?'

Sam nodded. He had his hands under the table. He didn't know yet how good this young feller might be, and he wasn't feeling all that special himself. Hell, he should never have come near the place. Being interrogated here by the fuzz was no part of his personal plan.

Eileen scurried off. Parker took the chair opposite Sam, and out came the note-book, and a friendly smile that was intended to put Sam at his ease.

'It's just a formality, sir – could I start with some details about yourself.'

'Yes,' said Sam, and in his most sincere style he said his piece as his brain ticked over rapidly. He was Frank Foster, currently residing at the 'Ocean View' caravan camp. On holiday. Occupation – wholesaler in fancy goods. Permanent address – 74, Little Casterford Road, Cambridge. So far it sounded all tidy and satisfactory and by the time they got round to checking it Sam intended to be far away.

Eileen brought the coffees and she didn't linger.

'Now what's it all about, officer?' said Sam, the honest tax-payer eager to assist the police.

'Didn't Eileen tell you?' said Parker.

'She said something about the Winters being missing, and that you were looking for them – is that it?'

'That is roughly the case,' said Parker. 'Mr and Mrs Winters, we are making enquiries as to their whereabouts, and I think you may be able to help me, Mr Foster.'

'Me?' said Sam. 'But I didn't really know them.'

'That is not quite the impression you gave Eileen,' said Parker, still pleasant.

Sam nodded. 'I see what you're getting at now.' So little Eileen had probably dropped him right in the dirt.

'Good,' said Parker briskly. 'She says you were interested in them, unusually so, and you say you didn't know them.'

'Well now,' said Sam, frowning, 'I remember I met them in the bar here a couple of nights back, and we got chatting, you know how it is, officer.'

D.C. Parker waited, offering nothing.

'You want the truth?' said Sam confidentially.

'It usually helps, sir.'

'I fancied Anne Winters,' said Sam. 'I mean, I'm down here on holiday, what the hell – I got the idea she might be interested, no crime in that, is there?'

Parker glanced at him. 'She was a married woman here with her husband, Mr Foster.'

Sam grinned. So let him think I'm a randy bastard. 'I hear she's pushed off with her husband, so I must have been wasting my time.'

'It would appear so,' said Parker acidly.

'Still, you can't win them all,' said Sam.

'You didn't by any chance arrange to meet her elsewhere?' said Parker.

'I didn't get that far,' said Sam ruefully. 'I mean, her old man was always hanging around, never gave me the chance to put it up to her... I didn't go much on him to tell you the truth. But she was a right smasher, she can park her shoes under my bed any time she likes.'

D.C. Parker had put his note-book away. Sam's lecherous enthusiasm plainly did not appeal to him, so maybe he was sweating on his Sergeant's stripes.

'I wonder why they skipped out like that?' said Sam.

'We expect to find that out,' said Parker. 'Exactly when did you see them last?'

'Must have been two nights ago,' said Sam. 'That's right, it was at dinner, and I sat at this table so that I could watch her over there, sort of romantic, know what I mean? They left before I did and they weren't in the bar afterwards because I looked.'

D.C. Parker stood up. 'How long will you be at the "Ocean View", Mr Foster?'

'Another ten days or so,' said Sam. 'Eileen says they didn't take any luggage with them.'

Parker nodded.

'Maybe they had an accident, got drowned, something like that? But I expect you've covered all that.'

'We have.'

Sam was uneasy at the thought that this fine upstanding young copper wasn't ready to come clean and tell him about the business yesterday at Poole with Phil Harrigan's cruiser. Poole would have told the local station. And the hotel manager must have reported last night's visit from Harrigan in search of Jerry Winters.

A crafty poker-faced young copper. You can get knotted, boyo. Sam smiled apologetically, and said, 'sorry I haven't been more help, officer. I hope you find them.'

'We expect to. I may be in touch with you again, Mr Foster.'

'Any time,' said Sam genially. 'Always ready to cooperate with you chaps, you're doing a grand job.'

D.C. Parker stared at him briefly, not quite sure the mickey wasn't being taken, but Sam's face was earnest and free from guile. Now shove off, copper.

Parker did just that, leaving Sam to pay for the coffee and happy to do so. There was no sign of Eileen yet, so he put some money on the table and left. He thought the girl in the hotel office was giving him a long hard look, and then he noticed Parker in the background, so he didn't linger for any more light chat, yakking with Eileen had landed him in enough trouble already.

And young Parker might recollect that he hadn't asked Sam to prove that he was this Frank Foster from Cambridge. When he got back to the station he was likely to get an earful from his boss, so hanging around the hotel wasn't going to do Sam any good at all.

It was second nature to him to make sure he wasn't being followed, and he dawdled along, inspecting the shops at his leisure, and looking out for Parker dodging after him. There hadn't been a police car outside the hotel when he arrived, if there had been he would never have set foot inside. Maybe Parker had used a plain car, or come on foot.

Would they check up with Cambridge? He hadn't given that young copper any reason to suspect that he wasn't what he said he was, had he? That had been a clever touch, pretending he'd been after Anne Winters, and in spite of the presence of her husband, that had disgusted young Parker all right. Put him right off. Still, you never could tell with the fuzz.

One thing was clear to Sam, this area was becoming too hot. It was sheer luck that he was still at liberty on this bright and sunny morning, and it was Sam's sad experience that luck had a nasty habit of running out at the wrong time.

By the time he reached the Viva he had

satisfied himself that there was nobody on his tail. He had been shadowed by real experts in his day, and there wouldn't be anybody at the local station smart enough to fool him. He was clean, temporarily.

He left the town by the side road and he felt in a brighter frame of mind, also temporarily. He had got out of a tricky situation. Most of his previous encounters with the police had ended with a brisk invitation to accompany them to the nearest nick, and that could easily have happened this time as well if young Parker had been a bit sharper and not taken in by Sam's Casanova stuff. Ambitious C.I.D. fellers shouldn't have moral principles, they got in the way of the job, Sam reflected. He had met plenty who wouldn't know a moral principle if it stood up and slapped them in the chops. Inspectors, Supers.

He drove to 'Ocean View', parked and packed all his gear. He could find a better place to roost. He stopped at the office by the entrance, where Harry Harding was working over some accounts, no doubt fiddling the figures.

'Morning, stranger,' said Harding cheerily. 'You must be getting your share somewhere, I never seem to see you around here in the evenings. The telly working okay now?'

'Haven't had the chance to try it yet,' said Sam. He put the key of his caravan on the counter, and said regretfully, 'I'm afraid I have to leave. I rang my office this morning, just to see how they're coping, it was the worst thing I could have done – they've got themselves into a tangle and I have to go back and sort it out – wouldn't it make you sick and just when I'm supposed to be on holiday and all!'

'That's rough,' said Harding. 'You don't expect you'll be back then?'

'Not very likely,' said Sam.

Harry Harding tugged his nose between finger and thumb.

'Sorry I can't do anything about a refund, company policy … my hands are tied.'

'I'm not worried about that,' said Sam.

Harding looked relieved. 'That's bad luck on you,' he said and made himself sound genuinely sympathetic. 'Shall I keep the caravan for you just in case?'

Sam appreciated Harding's private problem – if he could safely let the caravan again he increased his rake-off.

'Not a hope,' said Sam. 'You don't know my staff. When they cock a thing up they do it properly, it'll take me most of a week to straighten things out, I'm in export, the paper work can be tricky if you don't watch what you're doing. I'll try again later in the summer, look you up then, okay?'

'Sure,' said Harding. 'Give me a tinkle first and I'll have something laid on.' Man-to-man and in there pitching to the end.

Sam said he'd do that and took his leave. He headed for the Winchester Road and he moved along smartly. Choosing the New Forest district had been a mistake, but then he hadn't known he was going to run up against serious complications, like Phil Harrigan and the two Winters – he hoped they were in Dublin by now.

And there was Russell Colley, especially there was Russell Colley. He had some hours to put in before he thought about London. He had to work out a strategy for the evening. One thing was sure, it was going to pay a nice dividend – one thousand quid. It would double his working capital and give him even more room to move.

ELEVEN

Historic cathedral cities were not Sam's favourite territory. Just places to pass through on the way somewhere else. But Sam had to eat and there was no need to rough it in some roadside café. He parked the car in Winchester, and in a quiet side street came on a hotel that didn't advertise itself from the outside, but as soon as he went down the wide steps into the hall he knew he had guessed right. This was the place where county and upper-class landlords came for a nosh up – quality grub for quality people and to hell with the working stiffs. With cash in his pocket Sam was as good as the best of them.

It was late so there were tables to spare. Sam was escorted to a table and sat and examined the menu, as though he could read the French stuff.

A fat character in a black suit with a bit of a purple shirt showing under his clerical collar was at the next table, chomping away at his grub. A bishop or something important like that, Sam surmised. A cheery old geezer, spreading benevolence on one and all. He caught Sam's eye.

'Try the beef,' he suggested in a matey fashion. 'Always good here.'

It was practically a commandment from on high, an inside tip from one connoisseur of good grub to another, and as such not to be disregarded.

Sam said thanks very much and he would do as suggested. After all if you couldn't trust a bishop now who the hell could you trust? The reverend gent's advice turned out to be most sound.

Sam was just about the last to vacate the dining-room after an eminently satisfactory and quite expensive meal. He took coffee and a cigar and a snort of brandy in a sort of glass-roofed alcove with tall potted plants and a lot of genteel hush to aid digestion.

The clerical gent had anchored himself in a deep chair with a foot-rest; his hands were folded over his paunch, and he was having a nice zizz all to himself. A bloke like him must be on to a nice racket, Sam was thinking. Plenty of perks and the money couldn't be bad when you got enough rank.

Sam's acquaintance with the clergy was limited to prison chaplains and suchlike, and he had never given them much thought or taken them seriously because he had never reckoned they were on his wave length. Before he had finished his cigar, the bishop had come back to life, and as he came past Sam's chair he nodded and said, 'I was right, hey?' Then he steamed off, secure in his cosy world, and sure of the next. It takes all sorts.

It was a long afternoon, and Sam had the time to make his way towards London by easy stages. He stopped for a cup of tea at a café in Hounslow. He helped himself to a quick look at the London evening paper on the counter, and at last it was there in print: *Percy Cater.* He had been identified, and there was a picture of him taken a few years ago, blurry but still recognisable as Percy, and a brief digest of his criminal career; he was described as a skilful safe-blower, recently released from prison. The police were looking for a third party, so far not named.

Very carefully Sam put the paper back where he had found it, and there was nothing in his face to indicate that he felt as though somebody had just kicked him low in the belly. It was a lousy picture of Percy, but the name was there all right and he could just see Lily turning the paper over and seeing the picture and then reading the name.

Or some sharp-eyed bastard in one of the local shops Percy had used. But Lily was the real danger. That unnamed third party might even now have a name. And here he was riding back into London just where they would be looking for him. He would collect that thousand quid off Russell Colley and he wouldn't be in London any longer than the job took. Somewhere outside, Reading or Oxford, some place like that, tomorrow morning, he would do a little deal over the Viva – it was in good nick and he wouldn't ask much for it. He'd pay cash for something else, and the rest of the summer he could afford to hide out somewhere fresh, like Blackpool or Morecambe, plenty of people moving around up there and the whole place was new to him. So he wouldn't have to be dodging anybody.

He could pick up a bird and maybe rent one of those summer flats. The prospect cheered him considerably.

Feeling more nervous that he would have admitted to himself, promptly at seven-thirty he rang Domestic Developments, and Russell Colley said, 'Russell Colley speaking.'

'Nice,' said Sam. 'Right on the dot. You got the cash?'

'Yes.'

'Listen good,' said Sam, 'because I won't repeat it. Ten minutes from now, you come out of the building, turn right and start walking. Don't take a cab, just walk. Got that?'

'Yes, I understand.'

'I'll know if you're not alone,' said Sam, 'So don't try to be clever.'

'I'll be alone.'

'Ten minutes,' said Sam.

He was sitting in the Viva when he saw Russell Colley emerge and turn right as instructed; he was hatless and carried a black brief case, and Sam recognised him from the picture he had seen in the paper in that Bournemouth pub. There were some parked cars but they were all empty, and Russell Colley had that piece of the pavement to himself as he strode along, looking neither to right nor left.

When he came abreast of the Viva Sam opened the passenger's door, leaned across and said quietly, 'Mr Russell Colley, I believe,

191

hop in.'

Russell Colley's head swung round, he halted. 'In,' said Sam.

'Are you the man I've been talking to?' said Russell Colley.

'Nobody else,' said Sam. 'Don't let's hang around. In.'

Russell Colley got in, hugging that case. 'You have what we have been discussing?' he said stiffly.

'Be a bit crazy if I didn't,' said Sam. 'We'll take a little drive somewhere quiet and do a straight swap.'

'Why not here?' said Russell Colley.

'Think I'm daft?' said Sam. He was pulling the Viva out into the road. There was a squealing of tyres behind and a black Jaguar swung in from nowhere and Sam had to whip his wheel back to avoid being rammed.

'Stupid bastards!' he snapped.

The Jaguar had stopped, angled across the front of Sam's car so that he would have had to mount the pavement if he expected to proceed. The Jag's rear door was flung open and two large young men were advancing on Sam, clearly with no friendly intent. And in that moment Sam knew he'd been had for a sucker.

Already Russell Colley was scrambling out as Sam tried to slam into reverse. One of the young men leaned in and slapped him in the mouth.

'Let's have no fuss,' he said.

Sam wiped his mouth and tasted blood, his own blood, which did not encourage him to be heroic.

'To hell with this,' he said. 'What's the idea?'

By now Russell Colley had got into the back of the Jag, with that brief case. The young man who had done the slapping sat beside Sam and smiled at him. 'You've been clobbered,' he said politely. He was young and hard and nattily dressed in a dark suit. Sam didn't care for the way he was smiling; he was one of those handsome young fellers who'd be smiling politely while he cut your throat. His companion wasn't much better, just bigger; he had climbed into the back of the Viva so Sam felt surrounded and overwhelmed.

He glared at the black Jag squatting there in front. Russell Colley snug in the back.

'He set me up for this!' Sam's bitterness was heartfelt. 'I never thought he had the nerve!'

'You're playing with the big boys now,' said the one beside Sam. 'The rules are different, and you could never expect to win. Just follow the Jag like a sensible little chap. We wouldn't want any nonsense in public, would we?'

'You got me cornered,' said Sam. In the course of his career he had experienced the manifold vicissitudes of fortune, but he reckoned this had to be about the bottom of it all. Five minutes ago he had it all taped, now he was right back in the dirt.

The Jag was moving and Sam followed. His two passengers didn't say anything more to him, or to each other. They hadn't even bothered to search him to see if he had a gun – that showed real contempt. Just one slap in the mouth which hadn't done much damage.

To them he was nothing but trash, and it did him no good to be wishing that some violent and fatal things might happen to Russell Colley very soon. There was little traffic and the Jag was proceeding at a modest speed, so there was no difficulty in following it. At no time was Sam tempted to make a break for liberty when they were stopped by a red light, because he knew those two characters would love an excuse to duff him up.

They went south of the river, and when the procession finally turned into a pleasant tree-lined avenue in Wimbledon, Sam's insides began to churn: he was remembering that Phil Harrigan used to have a place around here, and he could see no kind of joy for him in the immediate future if Phil Harrigan had fixed all this.

He should never have touched any of this. He had eight hundred quid in the boot, and now he didn't fancy his chances to spend any of it. He was going to be a loser all round.

The Jag turned into the drive of a superior house with flower beds and lawns, dropped Russell Colley at the front door, and was then driven off. Colley hurried inside the house.

Sam braked the Viva by the door. The passenger in the front seat patted him on the shoulder. 'Very satisfactory, my little man.'

'Get stuffed,' said Sam morosely.

The young man took the keys of the Viva. 'Let's mind our language,' he said.

'Up yours,' said Sam. 'Kidnapping is a serious offence.'

'A delightful sense of humour,' said the young man, appealing to his companion in the back. 'Don't you agree, Henry?'

'It won't last, once we get him inside,' said Henry.

They didn't move, and Sam's uneasiness increased. They clearly were carrying out some kind of a plan. Sam examined the house and found nothing about it that he liked, flower beds and all.

His bladder began to bother him, he mentioned the matter and got no sympathy.

'Permission to smoke?' he said.

'Request refused.'

'What a lousy pair,' said Sam.

A man appeared at the door and beckoned. Sam was taken in through the hall and he was in no condition to note the tasteful decorations and the good furniture. Henry had a vicious and needless grip on his arm as though Sam had been putting up a strenuous resistance, while the other walked in front in case they lost their way.

Sam was shoved into a large room. Henry gave his arm a final and muscle-numbing squeeze. 'Here it is, gentlemen,' he said, and went out.

Phil Harrigan sat at a desk between two tall windows. He wore a dinner jacket and a frilly shirt and a dress tie that was just a little too floppy to go with his black beard. In one hand he held an unlit cigar, and on the desk in front of him was the case Russell Colley had been carrying. Russell Colley stood by the empty fire-place, and the two of them were giving Sam their best attention. Now there were just the three of them in the room, and Sam was the one doing all the sweating.

Harrigan's eyes were narrowed, and Sam felt they were ripping clean through him. The cigar invited him to approach nearer the desk, where the light from the windows would fall fully on his face.

'I know you,' said Harrigan softly. 'I know you don't I.'

Sam nodded, miserably.

'Don't tell me,' said Harrigan. 'I have the

name now – Sam Harris. Right?'

'Right,' said Sam.

Leaning back in his chair, Phil Harrigan lit his cigar, glanced across at Russell Colley, and said, 'Just an incompetent lump of rubbish who tried to sneak in some years ago, we threw him out. You've never seen him before?'

'Never,' said Russell Colley.

'Turn out your pockets,' said Harrigan. 'Put the stuff on the desk.'

The only item that interested Harrigan was Sam's wallet and the cheque he found inside it. 'Put the rest of your junk away,' he said, and Sam scooped up his small change and cigarette case, there was nothing else.

Harrigan spread the cheque out on the desk. 'Now, Sam Harris,' he said, 'you are in very bad trouble.'

'I know that,' said Sam, 'but I wasn't aiming anything at you, it was only that feller over there–'

'Blackmailing a Member of Parliament,' said Harrigan. 'You couldn't hope to swing a thing like that. I'm remembering your form, Harris – nicking stuff from parked cars, that's about your strength.'

Sam shrugged. 'I manage.'

'Not this time,' said Harrigan. 'How did you get hold of this cheque?'

'Jerry Winters gave it to me.'

Phil Harrigan slapped the desk with two

fingers and frowned. 'I want him, where is he?'

'Somewhere in Ireland,' said Sam. 'That's all I know, honest–'

'Let us keep your notion of honesty out of this,' said Harrigan. 'It will get us nowhere. Why did Winters give you the cheque?'

'I helped him out of a jam the night he set fire to those stables. If you look at it properly, I been on your side,' said Sam hopefully.

'Have you indeed?' said Harrigan. 'That is very interesting.'

'It's the truth,' said Sam.

Russell Colley stirred from his post by the fire-place. He came over and surveyed Sam from head to foot. 'What an abject specimen,' he said, very grand and contemptuous. 'Where on earth do you find them, Phil?'

'Just another reject,' said Harrigan.

'Now wait a minute,' said Sam. 'I don't get this – Winters told me you two had split up, that was why you sent him to do that dirty job on Colley's stables–'

'Perhaps there has been a change of policy,' said Harrigan.

'I see,' said Sam. 'So you're on the fiddle again–'

'We have declared an armistice,' said Harrigan. 'We have discovered that our mutual interests will be best protected by acting in concert on this occasion. You could say that you are the man who has brought this about, Sam Harris. To put it simply – we have agreed to deal with you between us.'

Phil Harrigan was smiling as he lifted the case, opened it up and shook it over the desk, nothing came out.

Russell Colley was watching Sam intently. 'You silly little man,' he said. 'Do you really imagine I was going to give you the money you had the impertinence to demand from me? You must be naïve.'

'It was worth a try,' said Sam. 'How was I to know you two chisellers were mates again?'

'You should have considered the possibility,' said Russell Colley like a lecturer with a dim audience. 'You decided to embark on a very dangerous course that was well beyond your ability; there were bound to be serious repercussions, even your limited intelligence should have told you that.'

'I don't like you much either,' said Sam. 'That makes us quits. The only difference is that you make a lot of money, and I'm struggling.'

'We have here an example of small fry trying to act big,' said Phil Harrigan. He took out his lighter, held up the cheque and set fire to one corner of it, and gently dropped it into a large glass ash-tray. The three of them watched it become grey ash.

'Well that takes care of me,' said Sam with assumed briskness. 'No harm done – okay if I go now? I won't be bothering you any more – that was the only cheque Jerry Winters got hold of... I thought I could turn it into cash – my mistake.'

Harrigan pointed to a chair by his desk. Sam sat on the edge of the chair because he now knew only too well that the interview was not over.

'Listen,' he said earnestly, 'I wouldn't try to pull anything on you–'

'I should hope not,' said Harrigan, amused at the very idea.

'It was just that bloke,' said Sam. 'I mean, he looked like an easy touch, and Jerry Winters said you were gunning for him – you can't blame me for trying, not in the circumstances, now can you?'

'The man's a complete moron, an imbecile,' said Russell Colley impatiently. 'We can believe nothing he tells us. I am waiting to hear you get the truth out of him.'

'You sound still nervous,' said Harrigan. 'You needn't be. I have been dealing with people like Sam Harris here for a long long time, and I always get what I am after.'

'That's right,' said Sam fervently. 'That's gospel.'

Russell Colley dropped into a chair, crossed one leg over the other, and the look on his face indicated that he thought the business rather beneath him.

There was a short silence. Sam fidgeted on the edge of his chair and tried to swallow saliva that wasn't there.

'There was only the one cheque,' he said. 'Honest to God, just that one, I didn't get anything else.'

'Nothing but sorrow,' said Harrigan softly.

He folded his hands together to make a rest for his chin. His cigar lay in that glass ash-tray, with the little wisp of ash that should have been worth a thousand quid to Sam.

'Okay, so I lost,' said Sam. 'That's about it—'

'I could wish another man sat where you are,' said Harrigan, 'and I don't have to tell you his name.'

'No,' said Sam dutifully. He could get glimpses of the nice evening outside through the windows behind Harrigan's desk, and he was wishing he was out there.

'I gave him a good break,' said Harrigan. 'If I had him here now instead of you, Harris, his wife would be a widow before the night was over, and you had better believe that.'

'I believe it all right,' said Sam with absolute sincerity.

'So now we come back to you,' said Harrigan. 'You got in out of your depth.'

'I didn't know you were backing that bloke

over there,' said Sam. 'I didn't know there'd been a switch–'

Russell Colley made a throaty sound.

'I got caught in the middle,' said Sam.

'An utter fool,' said Russell Colley venomously. 'Trying to blackmail me!'

'You're a high-class twister yourself,' said Sam.

Phil Harrigan was smiling, he seemed to be enjoying the spirited exchanges. He retrieved his cigar, found it was still alight, and went on smoking it, leaning back in his chair and with his hands linked behind his head.

Sam was encouraged to elaborate. He dredged into the recesses of his vocabulary and came up with some highly insulting stuff, until Russell Colley heaved himself out of his chair and for a moment Sam thought he was going to get himself belted.

And Harrigan thought so too because he said, 'let's cool it now.'

His well-fleshed face mottled with anger, like the squire addressing his bailiff over a defaulting tenant, Russell Colley snapped: 'I want him put where he can do no more damage – that is your province, Harrigan. I wish to know nothing about it!' Then he stalked out and slammed the door.

'There goes part of your meal ticket,' said Sam. 'Am I right?'

'Sam Harris,' said Harrigan, 'you know

too much and understand too little, that's a dangerous combination.'

'I'm not dangerous to you,' said Sam. 'I'm on my own, I don't have anybody to back me up, not a bloody soul – I do all my own sweating, and I don't know anybody I can trust with anything and that's a fact.'

'A loner,' said Harrigan, 'and you hoped to pull this off.'

'It should have worked,' said Sam gloomily.

'Now listen carefully,' said Harrigan with slow emphasis. 'The arrangement I had with the angry gentleman who has just left us was strictly private, and of no concern to anybody else. Understood? The worst mistake you could make was to imagine you could cut yourself a slice. That is the kind of thing I never allow.'

'I told you,' said Sam plaintively. 'I told you I didn't know you were interested.'

'If you had half a brain you'd know I had to be interested,' said Harrigan. 'It would never suit me to have any of those cheques getting into the wrong hands, even you can appreciate that. Which brings us to a matter we have yet to discuss, the letters I hear you have prepared–'

'That was just a bluff,' said Sam relieved at being able to give a prompt and truthful answer. 'I thought he'd buy it.'

'He had the good sense to get in touch with me,' said Harrigan. 'That was something else you should have taken into account. In the face of a common danger it was obvious that we would amalgamate, but you didn't think of that, and so here you are where you don't want to be.'

Harrigan's voice was gentle and reasonable. 'All on your own and right out of your depth. Do you think you have the nerve to bluff me and get away with it, Harris?'

Sam spread his sweating hands on his knees to keep them steady. 'God no,' he said passionately. 'I wouldn't even try!'

'I hope not,' said Harrigan. 'I have some young men who would love to work you over just by way of exercise. Russell Colley is a refined gentleman. I am not, as I imagine you must know. He dislikes even thinking of violence. I have no such inhibitions. To my way of thinking, the end justifies the means, and when I see that a mistake has been made I like to see it corrected. Now in your own muddled way you are quite an ambitious character. I suppose you must get some kind of a living, working on your own?'

Sam nodded. 'That doesn't mean I'd turn down a good offer if one came along.'

Phil Harrigan smiled faintly and shook his head. 'You're not getting one from me. I run a team, experts only. You know that. You would never fit in because you have nothing to offer. I made a mistake over Winters, not a mistake I intend to repeat, and I cannot afford outside interference, Harris.'

Here it comes, Sam thought unhappily. All that nice smooth talk, now the rough stuff. Phil Harrigan in his frilly shirt, puffing that fat cigar, about to embark on a civilised social evening somewhere, probably with that blonde bird Diana in some plushy club – Sam Harris was a minor inconvenience that would have to be taken care of before dinner.

'You won't be hearing any more from me,' said Sam hopefully.

'I'll be frank with you, Harris,' said Harrigan as though he really had Sam's welfare at heart. 'We clearly cannot have you running about with little pieces of information that might be damaging. It just isn't on. You present me with something of a problem. You are a loose end, and I always like to have a thing neatly tied up. So we have to do something about you.'

'I know when to keep my mouth shut,' said Sam with all the fervour at his command. 'You don't have to worry about me.'

'We must make sure of that,' said Harrigan pleasantly. 'You didn't expect to walk out of here, did you?'

He clicked on the inter-com on his desk. 'Send Henry in,' he said.

TWELVE

In desperation Sam gazed around that comfortably furnished room and found no comfort for himself anywhere. Certainly not in Harrigan's pitiless eyes that seemed to pin him to the chair, like a specimen ready for dissection.

The obedient Henry had arrived, soft of foot and quietly smiling, leaning by the closed door, his arms folded, waiting for instructions – enough to scare a braver man than Sam would ever be. Henry could break him into small pieces without raising a sweat.

'Listen,' said Sam quickly, 'just listen a minute, Phil–'

'The name is Mister Harrigan to you,' said Harrigan.

Sam ducked his head apologetically. 'I'm sorry,' he said, 'I didn't mean anything, Mister Harrigan–'

'I am remembering about you,' said Harrigan. 'Your wife divorced you and you have no family – correct?'

'Yes,' said Sam.

'So there is nobody who will miss you or mourn for you.'

'I wouldn't say that,' said Sam.

'So tell me who will miss you,' said Harrigan, smiling, as though they were playing some game and he had just scored a point.

'I got lots of friends,' said Sam, not at all happy at the way the conversation was going. 'I know plenty of people all over the place – I'll be missed all right.'

'If you will leave us their names and addresses we will see that they are suitably informed, if the need arises. We can't have your mates worrying about you, can we?' Harrigan inspected his cigar, it had gone out, he stubbed it vigorously in the ash-tray and shoved the ash-tray out of his way.

Sam had a singing in his ears and his bladder was giving him hell, and he couldn't see so well either.

'On the other hand,' said Harrigan thoughtfully, 'we could simply arrange for you to disappear without trace, I doubt very much if anybody will be concerned, except yourself, of course – but then you knew the risk you were taking when you stepped into my province. There's always a price, Harris.'

Sam drew a deep quivering breath. 'I been trying to explain,' he said in utter misery, 'but you don't want to believe me or listen to me. I was only after that Colley bloke… I can't do you any harm, so why lean on me, for God's sake?'

'You haven't been listening to me,' said Harrigan, 'or else you are a stupid little man

– you have a nuisance value, and I do not tolerate nuisances, so I get rid of them – must I spell it out more simply, Harris? I do not need you around, and that is final.'

Henry strolled over from the door, and stood looking down at Sam.

'There's not much of him, is there?' he said.

'That's Sam Harris,' said Harrigan. 'I want you to take him into the country, Henry, and give him the treatment.'

'Looks like he's crumbing already,' said Henry. 'Do I get serious with him?'

'Harris,' said Harrigan, 'how many cheques did Winters take?'

Sam pointed at the ash-tray. 'That was the only one, I swear it – just that one. He – he said he saw some of your bank statements, but that was the only cheque he got hold of, and that's the Gods truth. If there'd been any more cheques I'd have put the bite on Colley for more than a thousand, wouldn't I?'

'For such a little squirt you have big ideas,' said Harrigan. 'If you told me where I could put my hands on Winters you would do yourself a lot of good, you might even live a little longer.'

'All I know is that they're in Eire, they went this morning, they didn't tell me any more, but they won't be back, Winters is too scared–'

'I can believe that,' said Harrigan. 'If we can't have him we must make do with you.'

Sam's gaze swung unhappily from Harrigan to Henry and back again. He started to get up, as though he could plead more effectively on his own two feet. Henry placed a hand on Sam's shoulders and bounced him back into his seat and Sam felt the impact right up his spine.

Harrigan had Sam's wallet. 'You're rather flush, Harris,' he said, and with a great deal of pain Sam watched him empty the fivers out, Sam's spending money. 'I'll buy my boys a round of drinks from you,' said Harrigan and put the money in a drawer, smiling at Sam.

'You're welcome,' said Sam bitterly.

'He's all yours, Henry,' said Harrigan.

Henry hauled Sam to his feet. 'His car is still outside, do we use it?'

'Why not?' said Harrigan. 'He won't be needing it.'

Sam didn't care for the sound of that at all, but he was given no chance to voice any further protest. With more of that vicious grip on his arm, Henry propelled him out into the hall.

Diana was coming down the stairs, her blonde hair shining softly where the sun caught it through the landing window. She was moving like a beauty queen in a spotlight. Her dress was lime green and clinging to the point of indecency.

As she swayed past them in a cloud of provocative perfume without a glance at them, Henry said, 'Have fun, duckie.'

'Drop dead,' said Diana and went into Harrigan's room.

'Listen a minute,' said Sam pitifully, 'I have to use the toilet – have a heart...'

'Nothing to be ashamed of, Dad, that's just panic,' said Henry.

He whipped Sam across to a cloakroom by the stairs. He kept the door open and stood there while Sam made himself a little more comfortable. Then they went out to the car, waiting in the soft evening sunshine, and Sam had never felt so abandoned.

'Where are we going?' he asked.

'What an impatient little chap you are,' said Henry. 'You're going to drive, Sam. You're going to keep your eyes on the road and be ever so careful all the way, because I must tell you that I have a nasty temper when people upset me.'

They got into the car and Sam drove out into that respectable tree-lined avenue.

'We are going to a quiet little place in the country,' Henry said. 'We use it as a treatment centre for serious cases of disorder, like you, for instance. It has every amenity, very private and secluded.'

'Don't tell me I'm going to like it,' said Sam sourly.

210

'You won't,' said Henry. 'The full treatment is apt to get a little drastic, and you don't look all that rugged, if I may coin a phrase.'

'I get it,' said Sam. 'It's some bloody dump where you beat people up.'

'Phil Harrigan's firm does not encourage interlopers,' said Henry. 'It will be my pleasant duty to ensure that your nuisance value to us is nil in the future. You're driving very nicely Sam, keep it like that.'

'This is bloody murder!' Sam burst out. 'And it's all come about through a mis-understanding, it's all been a daft mistake, like I tried to tell Harrigan–'

'Mister Harrigan, if you please,' said Henry, interrupting. 'Everybody who comes unstuck says the same thing, and the jails are full of innocent men, we all know that. So don't squawk to me, Sam Harris, it won't help you now.'

'Listen,' said Sam, as coaxingly as he could, 'you don't look like any tearaway to me–'

'Nice of you to put it like that,' said Henry. 'For your private information, I used to be a medical student, and I can snap most of the bones in your body without leaving a bruise anywhere, which is why I was selected to accompany you to where you are going. Tell me, Sam, do you know anything about your threshold of pain? How much it takes to make you pass out? It can be a rewarding

211

study if you give it enough time and have the right apparatus.'

'You're just talking,' said Sam, but without any kind of conviction. 'You're trying to scare me, that's what – I don't believe Harrigan gave you any orders to knock me off...'

'Then we'll have to wait and see, won't we?' said Henry pleasantly. 'You must have been living in some kind of a dream world, Dad. Now you're up against the real thing and you're not going to enjoy it. You should have bolted with the other two.'

'I wish to God I had,' said Sam.

Under Henry's directions, and he seemed to know the road by heart, they were approaching Richmond, and Sam had decided that if he was going to try anything it would have to be done before they ran out of streets with people and traffic. Once they were out in the country he wouldn't have a hope, and at the end of the journey there was the prospect of having himself broken into little bits while Henry studied his threshold of pain and probably made scientific notes. Hell no, anything had to be better than that.

Passing the station they joined some fairly heavy traffic, and Sam had to slow down, and his face was the picture of misery. He had earlier suggested a brief stop at a pub for refreshment, and Henry had turned him down. The trip was to be non-stop, and one-way. Sam could smell his own sweat. The Viva was down to a walking pace behind a bus in the main street.

Henry surmised that Sam had something on his mind. He clamped one hand on Sam's thigh, his fingers probing for the muscles until Sam yelped with agony.

'I like the way you've been driving, Sam, so far. Just keep it going like that.'

'You damn near crippled me,' said Sam, rubbing his thigh, 'listen, did anybody search my car before we started?'

'What for?' said Henry, amused. 'Don't tell me we have a bomb on board?'

'Got something better,' said Sam quickly. 'There's over eight hundred quid in the boot, and Phil Harrigan doesn't know anything about it – so how do you like that?'

Henry's head swung round sharply. 'Where would you get eight hundred?'

'My last job,' said Sam. 'See for yourself if you like. It doesn't look like I'm going to get the chance to spend it, does it? I got an idea – you go a bit easy on me and we split it, Harrigan would never have to know – eight hundred mostly in fivers … take a look…'

They were coming up to the beginning of the Terrace, on their right was the busy bridge. Sam pulled in sharply, switched off and gave the keys to Henry.

'It's all wrapped in newspapers,' he said,

'under the tool kit.'

'Well I be damned!' said Henry in a whisper. 'You crafty little tramp!'

'I'll come with you if you like,' said Sam.

'You stay there or I'll break your neck,' said Henry, and got out.

They had stopped on the yellow lines in a very busy area and they would be in trouble quite soon. There were cars and buses lining up to cross the bridge on a lovely summer evening.

The moment Henry's head was out of sight as he bent to unlock the boot, Sam slipped silently out, darted into the stationary traffic, and began a nimble zigzag passage across the road, ducking low and keeping the vehicles between himself and Henry's view. He had never moved faster or with more agility in all his life.

One or two drivers bleeped at him. There was a bus stop opposite, and he just got to it when the traffic began to move. There was a bus loading up. He tacked himself on to the short queue, and clambered up to the top deck.

Henry stood on the pavement by the Viva. He had the parcel under his arm, the traffic was streaming past, and from the uncertain way Henry's head was swinging about it was obvious he didn't know which way Sam had gone. Before he slipped into a seat Sam saw Henry step out into the road and then get back in a hurry as a car nipped past. There were two other buses behind the one Sam was on, so if Henry worked it out he couldn't know which bus to follow, and he couldn't turn his car.

Sam took his seat and counted his change. It was less than a quid, and he had just said goodbye to eight hundred, the price of liberty. Henry would never have agreed to split with him and let him go. Phil Harrigan's mob didn't do private deals like that. They were too scared of Phil.

The bus rumbled back through Richmond. After that lightning dash Sam had regained his composure. He had no luggage and no bed for the night. He would have to organise something pretty fast if he didn't want to sleep rough, which was something he hadn't been obliged to do for a long long time.

No respectable joint would take him without luggage, and a flop-house would demand cash in advance. While he considered the problem he was watching out for a blue Viva, and he was continuing happy not to see it.

If the traffic hadn't been so thick at the bridge he would never have pulled it off. He lit one of his few remaining cigarettes. It had been expensive, but worth it and only a smart character like Sam Harris would have had the nerve even to try it, as Sam was pleased to admit to himself. They wrote him

215

off too soon, Phil Harrigan and his mob; they thought he was just a piece of trash to be pushed around and given the 'treatment' in that quiet country hideout.

Harrigan would blow his stack when he heard, and Sam enjoyed the mental picture he had of Henry trying to explain to Harrigan just how he'd been diddled on the roadside.

Twice he changed bus routes, and each time he reckoned he exhibited considerable finesse in satisfying himself that nobody was taking any hostile interest in his movements. Ice-cool nerve in a crisis: Sam Harris. Temporarily skint, maybe.

He finished up on the Underground, and emerged at Clapham South where the shades of night were falling. In a neighbourhood pub he bought himself a large whisky and drank it neat. It made a grievous dent in his capital, but it gave him some of the old zip he knew he was going to need.

He rang her from a call-box, and as soon as she heard who it was she broke in with some spirit:

'Why, Sammie,' she exclaimed. 'And where in the world have you been? I've been worrying myself sick, wondering where you were–'

'I'm okay,' he said quickly. 'The business thing got a bit tangled up–'

'I should hope it did!' she said. 'Three

whole days and not a word from you! It's a bit much, Sammie!'

'I'm sorry, Lily,' he said. 'I meant to phone, honest, but I got all tied up. It was a lousy trip – everything all right with you?'

'Well I don't know so much,' she said, still nursing her grievance. 'I mean, I saw you'd taken most of your clothes, so you can imagine what I've been thinking, especially when I didn't hear from you, I thought you'd left me for good, and that friend of yours, Percy Cater, he cleared his room out as well, not that I was sorry to see him go. But you, Sammie – it hurt me and I won't pretend it didn't, after all we'd been to each other, just clearing out without a word–'

'Lily, baby,' he interjected softly, 'it wasn't like that – you don't think I'd leave you?'

'What else was I to think?' she said with asperity.

'I should have explained before we left,' said Sam. 'I wasn't sure how long we'd be away, so I just packed all the clothes I thought I might need. I should have told you, Lily, it was thoughtless of me...'

'It really upset me,' she said.

'I'm sorry, baby,' he said, and he put in all the sincerity he could scrape up.

'It wasn't very nice, Sammie.' She was softening.

'I wouldn't do anything to hurt you,' he said. 'You mean too much to me.'

'Well then,' she said. 'Perhaps I did jump to the wrong conclusion, Sammie.'

'I couldn't blame you if you did,' he said. If she had seen Percy's picture in the paper she would have said something about it by now, Lily would never be able to keep a thing like that to herself.

'To tell you the truth,' she said confidentially, 'I began to have some pretty unfriendly thoughts about you, Sammie.'

Sam felt that cold shiver down the small of his back.

'Y'know,' she went on, 'I actually thought you might have a woman up there.'

Sam laughed, a genuine laugh. 'Baby, you couldn't be more wrong. You're the only one for me.'

'I wish I could believe you.'

Sam caught the wistful tone of her voice and knew he was in the finishing straight.

'Listen,' he said gruffly, 'there's nobody in the world more important to me than you are.' She would never know that for once he was giving her the absolute truth.

'Sammie,' she said softly.

'If it's any consolation to you,' he went on, 'the trip has been a disaster all round, a proper shambles.'

'No! You poor old thing!' Instant sympathy. It couldn't be better. 'But what went wrong?'

'Just about all of it,' he said. 'I won't bore

you with the details, but first of all, Percy Cater and I have split up.'

There was a pause. Then she said, 'I'm not sorry to hear that, Sammie. I never thought he was any good for you.'

'I even had to flog the car to cover my expenses,' he said. 'Those Brummie boys took me to the cleaners all right. I expect it was my own fault, trying to take on too much.'

He was giving it just the right touch of manly pathos.

'Oh Sammie,' she said, and now he had her really on her bended knees for him.

'I just thought you ought to know how things had turned out,' he said. 'I should have rung you before, I suppose I didn't like admitting I was a flop, a failure – not to you, Lily–'

'Sammie,' she broke in abruptly, 'where are you now?'

'Just up the road,' he said. 'But if you don't want to see me again I'll understand–'

'Silly man,' she said. 'Hurry home and I'll have supper ready.'

Sam got out of the call-box and wiped his face. It wouldn't have to be a bench in the park for the night.

Hurry home: that surely meant she hadn't heard about Percy Cater. Sam Harris, he told himself, you may be a conniving so-and-so, but you get the luck in the end.

At first Lily gave him a subdued welcome, almost matronly in fact, except that any mother who behaved as she eventually did would find herself in court. The whisky after supper mellowed both of them. She didn't press him with any awkward questions, and Sam gave her an imaginative and circumstantial version of his commercial misfortunes in the jungles of Birmingham, and he felt it was as good as any story he had ever put across.

The only time Lily mentioned Percy Cater was when she repeated that she was glad he had gone, and she wouldn't be letting his room again because it was much more cosy with just the two of them, wasn't it? And Sam had to agree.

Later that night, on the bedside table, her bedside table, Sam noticed the evening paper, folded so as to show that picture of Percy Cater, and placed where Sam had to see it.

Lily lay back on her pillows, her eyes fixed on Sam's startled face, and her smile was one of quiet triumph.

She patted the space on the bed beside her, 'There's nothing to worry about now, Sammie,' she murmured. 'It's just you and me. You came back and I don't care about anything else.'

'Have you told anybody?' His voice was thick and wobbly.

'Why should I? I never really liked him. And you didn't kill him, did you?'

'No,' said Sam. 'And I didn't make any money out of it either.'

Lily laughed softly. 'That was a lovely story you told me about Birmingham, Sammie. One day you must tell me what really happened.'

With particular vividness Sam was recalling a certain conversation with the late Percy Cater, when Percy had been warning him that he was in imminent danger of getting himself hooked by Lily, and Sam had been so sure he could look after himself.

He had walked slap into it, and old Percy could be laughing at him now.

Lily crooked a finger at him. 'Come and be nice to me,' she whispered. 'I'm waiting, Sammie.'

And as Sam climbed dutifully into her bed he was thinking that it might have been one hell of a lot worse. So why complain? Let battle commence.

The publishers hope that this book has given you enjoyable reading. Large Print Books are especially designed to be as easy to see and hold as possible. If you wish a complete list of our books please ask at your local library or write directly to:

Dales Large Print Books
Magna House, Long Preston,
Skipton, North Yorkshire.
BD23 4ND

This Large Print Book, for people
who cannot read normal print,
is published under the auspices of

THE ULVERSCROFT FOUNDATION